RETREAT FROM OBLIVION

Herb and Jean Hervey fight all the time. It makes him crazy, but still Herb can't get Jean out of his system. Jean's in love with Paul, Wilda's husband. All Paul wants to do is leave for China and become a flyer. One evening Herb meets Dorothy, whose husband Tommy is fighting in Spain. Dorothy wants comfort and company, and Herb can't keep away from her.

Then Jean lets herself get picked up by George Green, who can't keep away from *her*. It all adds up to a lot of trouble. *Retreat from Oblivion* is a story of passion, sacrifice and frustration set in New York City at the outset of World War II. It is a story you will not soon forget.

"Goodis has an originality of naturalism…
a creatively compelling vividness of detail."
—*San Francisco Chronicle*

David Goodis Bibliography
(1917-1967)

Novels

Retreat from Oblivion (1939)
Dark Passage (1946)
Nightfall (1947; reprinted as *The Dark Chase*, 1953; *Convicted*, 1954)
Behold This Woman (1947)
Of Missing Persons (1950)
Cassidy's Girl (1951)
Of Tender Sin (1952)
Street of the Lost (1952)
The Burglar (1953)
The Moon in the Gutter (1953)
Black Friday (1954)
The Blonde on the Street Corner (1954)
Street of No Return (1954)
The Wounded and the Slain (1955)
Down There (1956; reprinted as *Shoot the Piano Player*, 1962)
Fire in the Flesh (1958)
Night Squad (1961)
Somebody's Done For (1967)

Screenplays

The Unfaithful (with James Gunn, 1947)
The Burglar (1957)

RETREAT FROM OBLIVION
David Goodis
Introduction by Cullen Gallagher

Stark House Press • Eureka California

RETREAT FROM OBLIVION

Published by Stark House Press
1315 H Street
Eureka, CA 95501, USA
griffinskye3@sbcglobal.net
www.starkhousepress.com

RETREAT FROM OBLIVION
Originally published and copyright © 1939 by E. P. Dutton & Company, Inc., New York.

Reprinted by permission of the David Goodis estate. All rights reserved under International and Pan-American Copyright Conventions.

"But Is It Noir? The Deep, Dark Passages of *Retreat from Oblivion*"
© 2024 by Cullen Gallagher

ISBN: 979-8-88601-110-4

Book design by Mark Shepard, shepgraphics.com
Proofreading by Bill Kelly

PUBLISHER'S NOTE:
This is a work of fiction. Names, characters, places and incidents are either the products of the author's imagination or used fictionally, and any resemblance to actual persons, living or dead, events or locales, is entirely coincidental.
Without limiting the rights under copyright reserved above, no part of this publication may be reproduced, stored, or introduced into a retrieval system or transmitted in any form or by any means (electronic, mechanical, photocopying, recording or otherwise) without the prior written permission of both the copyright owner and the above publisher of the book.

First Stark House Press Edition: October 2024

7
"But Is It Noir? The Deep, Dark
Passages of *Retreat from Oblivion*"
by Cullen Gallagher

17
RETREAT FROM OBLIVION
By David Goodis

"But Is It Noir? The Deep, Dark Passages of *Retreat from Oblivion*"

by Cullen Gallagher

If you're reading this introduction, chances are you had a much easier time tracking down David Goodis's debut novel *Retreat from Oblivion* than practically anyone since it was initially published in 1939 by E.P. Dutton & Company, Inc. For upwards of 80 years, *Retreat from Oblivion* has been the author's rarest novel. Even some of his most ardent fans hadn't read it, or even set sights on a copy. Over the years, its scarcity only added to its allure—and when it comes to allure, few noir authors have as much of it as Goodis. There's something about his prose that draws people in, like a siren's dark song. I've heard the same complaints *ad nauseam* from the naysayers over the years—the plots don't make sense, he's too depressing, there's no mystery—obviously they didn't hear the siren.

In the early 2000s, it wasn't uncommon to see copies for sale listed at over $1000, far too rich for my blood. Since then, the price has only gone up. Luckily, close to twenty years ago, I found a lending library in Arizona that had it, and they were willing to send it via interlibrary loan to New York City, and I dropped a lot of quarters into a photocopier bootlegging it. That was later rephotocopied and given to a couple friends, and eventually it was scanned as a PDF. Who knows how far it traveled, or how many more generations of copies were made?

Truth be told, I never thought I would live to see the day this book would be reprinted. Because—

Retreat from Oblivion is not a crime novel...

Think about the publishers who have brought Goodis back into the limelight after his death in 1967, at age 49, when none of his works were in print (his last novel, *Somebody's Done For*, was still a few months away from publication). He has always been associated with crime imprints. The publishing renaissance of his work began in the 1980s, in the UK with Zomba Books's "Black Box Thrillers" and Simon & Schuster's Blue Murder, and in the US, with Black Lizard. Even after Black Lizard was sold to Vintage, they stuck with the gritty titles. In the late-90s, Serpent's Tail had a "Midnight Classics" line. After the turn of the millennium, Serpent's Tail returned to Goodis in 2006 with *Black Friday and Selected Stories* (edited by Adrian Wootton); Hard Case Crime republished *The Wounded and the Slain;* and the Library of America included *Down There* in *Crime Novels: American Noir of the 1950s*, before honoring him with *Five Noir Novels of the 1940s And 50s*. Centipede Press (and its imprint Millipede), known primarily for horror, reissued *Nightfall* and *Street of No Return*.

The common element in these publishers?

Crime. Mystery. Darkness. Noir.

It's understandable why these publishers didn't touch *Retreat from Oblivion*. It didn't fit their image. If you're a fan of *Nightfall*, or *Dark Passage*, or *Down There,* or—well, any other Goodis novel, then you might be expecting some sort of mystery, some sort of nefarious narrative, definitely a life-threatening situation, maybe some thieves, gangsters or cops ... something criminal, whatever it may be! Honestly—it was probably for the better that those publishers didn't touch this book, because Stark House Press is the perfect place for *Retreat from Oblivion*. Stark House has devoted itself to not only keeping Goodis in print (with a trio of *Nightfall / Cassidy's Girl / Night Squad*, and *Somebody's Done For*) but also many other of his fellow pulp and paperback comrades, giving it their work historical context and critical consideration they rarely received in their lifetime.

Retreat from Oblivion is not a crime novel...

If *Retreat from Oblivion* isn't a crime novel, then what is it? Journalists and marketing writers at the time seemed divided on how to describe it. Romance? Socio-political? Political diatribe? War story? International epic?

"A love story of modern Americans in their thirties."—*New York Herald Tribune* ("Books Received," June 25, 1939, pg. H16).

"A cross-section of young Americans caught in the political and social upheaval of this era."—*New York Herald Tribune* ("Book Notes," June 30, 1939, pg. 17).

"A picture of young people in their thirties who fight for democracy and freedom."—*New York Times* ("Book Notes," June 26, 1939, pg. 18)

"A story of modern America—with its many characters battling out their individual problems of life and love behind a background of world chaos."—*The Jewish Exponent* ("Local Author Publishes First Novel," July 7, 1939, pg. 7)

"The story of a group of shoddy people whose destinies are controlled by warfare in China and Spain."—Rose Feld, *New York Times* ("Love Affairs," July 16, 1939, pg. 74)

Frankly, I think they all got it wrong.

The best way I can describe *Retreat from Oblivion* is as a modernist melodrama—a tad heavier on the melodrama than the modernism, but it still has the hallmarks of that literary movement (a fragmentary narrative, jumping from character to character, in and out of their heads, occasionally slipping into stream of consciousness inner-monologs, and even cross-cutting between romance and war genres like two reels from different movies interspliced). Like Hemingway before him, Goodis searches for poetry in brutality, barbarism, and barrooms, and his male characters are haunted by their failure to live up to their own idealized standards of masculinity, and frequently express their existential anguish through violence and self-destruction.

The story centers around ad man Hebert Hervey, who is bored with his job and trapped in a marriage, neither of which he cares much about. At work, his eyes are drawn to the figure of his secretary, Helen Gillen, onto whom he also hoists more of his work responsibilities. At home, his wife Jean is carrying on with a couple of affairs, including E. George Green (ex-college athlete, presently unemployed lawyer) and Paul Schuen, an airplane engineer and Herb's best friend. Paul, meanwhile, is married to Wilda, who is doing everything in her power to convince Paul not to run off to China to be a volunteer pilot in their war against Japan. It's not long before Jean realizes she is pregnant, and runs off with Paul to China. Wilda is crushed. While wandering through Harlem, Herb meets Dorothy, a factory worker whose husband, Tommy, is currently overseas fighting in the Spanish Civil War with the Republicans against the Nationalists. Because of Tommy, Herb is uncomfortable pursuing the relationship, and instead focuses his attention on Helen.

Such is the tangled web which Goodis wove for his tormented cast of characters. Lovers. Fighters. Dreamers. Drunkards. The downtrodden and the depressed. Loners. Losers. Cheaters. Haunted by their past. Hopeless about their future. Dissatisfied by their present. You could say the same about the characters in most of his stories and novels for the rest of his career—and, in that sense ...

Retreat from Oblivion is not a crime novel ... but it is noir.

This book is pure Goodis, and his melancholic-noir poetry is on full display from the very first sentence (which is later reprised for the last chapter).

> After a while it gets so bad that you want to stop the whole business. You figure that there's no use in trying to fight back. Things are set dead against you and the sooner you give up the better. It's like a mile run. You're back there in seventh place and there isn't a chance in the world. The feet are burning, the lungs are bursting, and all you want to do is fall down and take a rest.

The words—straight from the forlorn subconscious of Herb—reverberate throughout the rest of Goodis's career. It's practically his manifesto, and it could easily appear in any of his later novels. Even in the midst of aviation pulp stories, between dodging Nazi bullets and downing Japanese Zeros, Goodis's pilots evoke the ad man's despondent plea: "For a moment he was tempted to jump in a plane, give it the gun, and fly the hell away from the whole business" ("Bullets for Nazis," *Captain Combat*, June 1940). "He had done his best, but now he felt sick and tired of the entire business and he didn't care what they did with him" ("Wings of the Cobra, *Fighting Aces*, May 1944).

Other moments from the book, too, echo throughout many future works. Herb and Jean anticipate many cheating couples to come, especially the fraught marriage between Vincent and Gert in *Dark Passage*. The scene in which Jean fuels a vicious fist-fight between Herb and George would be reworked in "The Devil Keeps a Woman" (*Ten Story Gang*, August 1939, published just a month after *Retreat* hit the shelves). Gangster Dino Vocco is making the moves on his number-two Danny Laducci's gun-moll, Nita Terriss. When Danny comes home and catches the two of them together, Nita goads the two alphas in a knock-down-drag-out-fight as they exercise the most destructive (and self-destructive) aspects of their masculinity. Nita, like Jean before her, is less interested in love than control. In this light, Jean from *Retreat* is the mold from which all of Goodis's future *femmes fatale* would spring (its more pure expression is, arguably, Clara in *Behold This Woman*).

This was only his first novel, but already Goodis had his trademark sensibility, a style and a sentiment that would follow him throughout his stories and novels, through aviation adventures and sports games, and down desolate alley ways, like a relentless Philadelphia wind. Consider a passage like this, when Jean informs Paul that she is carrying his baby:

> Her eyes were filmed now with a luster that thickened and then receded, so that the light of the room was reflected in them like star beams upon a dark pool. And her lips parted slightly, her arms came out from beneath the cover and went up to him. As always he was lost, bewildered, and then completely overwhelmed, like a helpless swimmer in a rip tide, taken out slowly, stunned by the bounding breakers, then pulled out with ever increasing swiftness until the tide slackened and there was nothing more but the depths beneath,

the surrender, a clutching arm slowly covered by the water.

Moments before, Jean had told him, "I don't feel bad about it. I don't think I've ever been happier." And here is Paul, looking into her eyes and seeing fantasies of drowning. Water is a central metaphor to Goodis's fiction, notably at the end of *The Burglar* and at the start of *Somebody's Done For*, and in many of the aviation stories like "Wings of the Cobra" (*Fighting Aces*, May 1944), where pilots float in the water, torn between the desire for death and the struggle for life. The River Styx separates the shores of the living and the dead, but in Goodis mythology it is the surface of the ocean that separates the two realms:

> The Cobra was going down, taking him down there into the dark and glutinous green caverns of the tremendous ocean—and he couldn't move his leg. Pain gripped his lungs and he wanted to relax and exhale and let the Cobra take him down to the bottom of the Pacific." "Wings of the Cobra" (*Fighting Aces*, May 1944)

Among the most unusual aspects of *Retreat from Oblivion* are its intercut combat scenes, first with Tommy in Spain and later with Paul in China. More than just an invocation of Ernest Hemingway as a literary model, Goodis uses these scenes as a physical and metaphoric expression of his characters' fears and desires. Tommy joins out of a sense of political duty, and Paul dreams of escaping his drab life and experiencing ecstasy in the air. But this is noir, or proto-noir if you will, where nobody finds what they are looking for—instead of feeling patriotic, Tommy badly wants to abandon his post and return to Dorothy; and Paul's past literally follows him when Wilma comes looking for him. These character types will appear time and again in future works. Paul is the first of Goodis's aviators who seek redemption in the sky for their earthly sins. And though we don't spend as much time with Tommy as other characters, he exhibits a vulnerability and frailty that will be developed in future characters: he is the first of many whose dreams will be smashed by life's cruelty.

Retreat may mark the first publication appearance of Goodis's interest in aviation, but it was a long-held interest of his, and would continue to inspire his pulp fiction for many years to come. For his debut novel, he paid particular attention to this aspect of the story, and tried to make it as realistic as possible:

> The battle scenes in *Retreat from Oblivion* are based on actual incidents in the Spanish and Chinese conflicts. Although Goodis admits he was not in close contact with these engagements, he did interview several returned volunteers in order to gain authentic military information. A thorough student of the subject, Goodis won honors in a course in military strategy while at Temple. Since then he has made more or less a hobby of modern military art, and recently wrote a play based on historical and technical research he made on the Battle of Tannenberg. It is now being read by a New York producer."—*The Jewish Exponent* ("Local Author Publishes First Novel," July 7, 1939, pg. 7)

Ultimately, what makes *Retreat from Oblivion* so distinctly noir is the sense of sadness that graces each page, and in spite of many comic scenes in the novel, underscores every character action and motivation:

> Sometimes a guy gets filled with a heavy sadness that is suddenly covered over by a grin and a laugh. And then over that there comes another sadness, something fine and beautiful that can't be explained. It just exists there. And over this there comes another grin and another laugh. Sometimes it just keeps up this way. There is this pain, and then there is this laugh. And above it all there is a big question mark.

Herb and company are the first group of motley mopers in Goodis's literary universe—people trapped in a world they feel powerless to change. Herb looks for real love. Jean looks for thrills. Wilda wants affection. Paul wants excitement. George wants easy money. Dorothy and Tommy are idealists who want a better world. Most of these characters don't get what they want. For a 22-year-old, Goodis is already quite jaded. But, seeing as it's his first book, there's a glimmer of hope at the end. I'm just warning you now don't give up when things look bleakest.

Reviewers at the time mostly disliked the book. Even the faint praise of John Patton in the *New York Herald Tribune* was given with reservation. Other critics, like Patton's colleague Lisle Bell, had no reservations about their negative judgment:

> "It is unfortunately realistic, typical of a certain stratum in American life, and faithfully written in the jargon of that stratum. If the artistry is judged conscious, it is a good piece of work. If not, it is utterly insignificant, proving nothing but that the stratum does not offer a pretty picture."—E.B., *Los Angeles Times* ("Triangles Make Unlovely Picture," July 16, 1939, pg. C6)

> "There is a good deal of drinking and beating up of men and women on this side of the two oceans and some synthetic fighting across them. In his efforts to be dramatic Mr. Goodis occasionally writes a sentence like this one: 'George tightened his lips and curled one over his lower teeth, pressing it with the upper.'"—Rose Feld, *New York Times* ("Love Affairs," July 16, 1939, pg. 74)

> "In the early-Greenwich-Village-late-imitation-Hemingway style, which is saved from its own oblivion not only by the author's clever streamlining, but by the satiric savagery in his hatred for the worthless characters of his creation. To be sure, Mr. Goodis falls into the not uncommon error of confusing devotion to a cause with personal nobility, and his Dorothy, who is the book's heroine, is as neurotic, and almost as uncontrolled, as his Jean, who is its evil spirit ... This is a callow and theatrical, as well as an ugly and brutal book: but there seems to be a kind of raging earnestness in the author's mind."—John Patton, *New York Herald Tribune* ("Books and Things," July 17, 1939, pg. 9)

> "His people are very amorous and drunken. There is almost always a bottle or a bar handy, and the boys and girls imbibe freely... It might be tragic, but these people are just weaklings. The advertising end is probably authentic. Mr. Goodis should know that."—Sidney Williams, *Philadelphia Inquirer* ("'Black

Narcissus' Is Tale of Missionaries in India," July 19, 1939, pg. 16)

"The opening sentence in *Retreat from Oblivion* is as follows: 'After a while it gets so bad you want to stop the whole business.' It refers to Herb's state of mind, but it's also not an inaccurate summary of what one is inclined to say about David Goodis's novel."—Lisle Bell, *New York Herald Tribune* ("New Popular Novels," July 30, 1939, pg. H9)

Reviewers at the time saw it as yet another debut in an overcrowded field. They focused on its shortcomings, its clichés, its naiveté. Reading it in 2024, we can see it for something else. Instead of trying to guess *where the author's career was headed*, and can look back and see *where it all began*.

David Goodis was always David Goodis, always stumbling down streets of the lost, streets of no return, forever trapped in dark passages, and always retreating from that incessant sense of oblivion.

—July 2024

....

Cullen Gallagher is a musician and writer living in Brooklyn, NY. He is the author of *Looking for Lost Streets: A Bibliographic Investigation of David Goodis's Pulp Fiction* (Pulp Serenade Press, 2024), and the forthcoming critical companion *High Fliers, Middleweights, and Lowlifes: David Goodis in the Pulps* (Pulp Serenade Press). He has written essays for many Stark House Press books, including volumes by W.R. Burnett, Day Keene, Ed Lacy, Peter Rabe, Lionel White, and Harry Whittington. His non-fiction has appeared in the *Los Angeles Review of Books* and the *Paris Review*, as well as the anthologies *Paperbacks at War: 20th Century Conflict from the Front Lines of Vintage Paperbacks, Pulps and Comics* (2021), *Screen Slate: New York City Cinema 2011-2015* (2017), and *Cult Cinema: An Arrow Video Companion* (2016). He is also the co-author (with Kevin L. Stoeher) of *King Vidor in Focus: On the Filmmaker's Artistry and Vision* (McFarland Books, 2024).

RETREAT FROM OBLIVION

David Goodis

CHAPTER I

After a while it gets so bad that you want to stop the whole business. You figure that there's no use in trying to fight back. Things are set dead against you and the sooner you give up the better. It's like a mile run. You're back there in seventh place and there isn't a chance in the world. The feet are burning, the lungs are bursting, and all you want to do is fall down and take a rest.

He was sitting in the office and he had a lot of work to do. But he couldn't get started. He was just sitting there trying to figure it all out. And he felt this way. He wanted to give up. He wanted to fall asleep for good.

One of the girls came over and gave him some copy. He took it and then looked at her. She was a good kid. She never had much to say. He wondered how much trouble she had seen. It was a funny question to ask people. How much trouble do you have? Do you have half as much as I have?

He began to work on the copy but his mind would not direct his fingers. The papers were put away to the right of the desk. He just sat there. In a few minutes he got up and looked out the window.

Things were pretty bad. They were getting worse each minute.

"Mr. Hervey."

"Yeah." He did not turn around.

"There's someone here to see you, Mr. Hervey."

"Who?"

"Your wife."

"What does she want?" He turned around.

"She wants to see you."

"Tell her to wait a minute."

The girl went out. He stood there waiting for Jean to come in.

This was going to be good. He wondered what had happened to make her come around. The split had started two weeks ago at a party, when she had called him a few hundred names, had thrown a glass of ginger-ale highball in his face and then, after he hit her, had tried to kick him in the stomach. After that he figured it was over for good. He could never kiss anything like that again.

Now she was here and she was coming into the office. "Hello, Herbert."

"Hello."

Jean was doing all right. She could model for face and she could model for body. And she could wear clothes. She could spend money and she could eat your heart out. That was about all she could do. He looked her over and asked himself why he was not excited looking at her.

"Well?" she said.

"What do you want me to do, throw myself all over you?"

"Oh."

"What's on your mind?"

"Just this," she said. "I'd like to know what your plans are."

"I have no plans." He was talking slowly, but he was not hesitating. "If this business is okay with you it's okay with me. You don't see me worrying, and I don't think you've been spending the last two weeks crying your eyes out either."

"How long is this going to last?"

He waved an arm at her disgustedly, and he twitched his tongue. "It's been lasting ever since I laid eyes on you. It'll last as long as we know each other. When I don't see you I—" No, he figured. He closed his mouth and forced the words back down his throat. That was something he would never tell her. Maybe she knew it already. But he would never tell her.

"When you come back to the apartment tonight I'll be there," she said.

It was pretty smooth, the way she got away with that one. She let the words slide out of her lips, and her eyes were hazy. She leaned a little on one foot, and he got dizzy looking at her. When it was like this he could hardly talk.

While he was still trying to get out of it and say something smart, she twisted slowly, and sort of flowed out of the office.

Herb went back to the desk. There was a bottle of Scotch, unopened, in the second drawer, but he got a hold on himself and determined to leave it alone. Once he got his mouth on that bottle, he would probably finish it.

The whole business flipped before him like a pack of cards. At the beginning it had come close to being beautiful. His old man had plenty of money, and had sent him to Columbia. He finished three years and then quit. It was on account of a girl, some lovely sweet kid who was too dumb to live. She didn't even want to marry him. He tried to make things work out, but she was really too dumb. It had to be broken up. Then the old man had gotten disgusted with him. He got him a job in an advertising agency and Herb messed things up there too. He was out of work for a year. He nearly went crazy figuring out things to take up time. He started to play baseball with a sandlot outfit and he could field a ground ball.

But by this time he was twenty-five and sandlot baseball was no money. Besides, he was drinking a lot and he was very far from being happy. The guys on the team were his own age and older, and they had little or no brains. He asked his father to send him back to school.

After he graduated he took the postgraduate course in journalism and that was another year. From then on it had been a steady succession of jobs and no work, jobs and no work. He quit more times than he was fired. A newspaper routine was unbearable.

And all this time it was a matter of searching for something and perhaps someone.

So finally, a year after he got this job in the advertising agency, he met Jean. For four months he rushed her. Then they were married.

Now, they had been married three years. Here he was, thirty-two, and she was twenty-nine. Here he was, and he figured he wasn't by any means the meanest dog in the world. At least, when a man analyzes his own actions on a factual basis rather than by shallow egoism, the result should show a reasonable degree of truth. And the facts showed that he was not cheap, in fact he was a spendthrift. And his temper did not rise easily, he could keep it in fairly well. He tried hard not to be boring. When he really had nothing to say he made it a point to keep his mouth shut.

Sitting here and figuring all this out, he had to laugh. He was just wasting time throwing bouquets at himself and trying to make her out as a cobra. Besides, it was three o'clock and he had a lot of work to do. He shifted himself in the chair and bent over the desk.

After she left the office Jean took in a movie on Seventh Avenue and left when it was three-quarters over. She got in a taxi and went back to the apartment. When she was nearly there she wished that she had stayed in the center of town. But then the cab was going fast and while she wondered what to do next the driver pulled up at the apartment house.

They had an orange and white set of rooms on the third floor. The parlor was big and fairly high. There was a white rug and an orange piano. That had been her idea, and it had started one of their fights. They still argued about it occasionally when they had nothing else to do.

She picked up the phone and called Wilda.

"What are you doing?"

"Dying a slow death," said Wilda. "I just got finished a half-hour's talking with Paul. I had an awful time with that fool, Jean. I'm worried about him, honest to God I am."

"What did he say?"

"Oh, he called up and begged me to talk with him. He said that if I didn't talk to him real fast and didn't say the things he wanted me to say, he was going to leave."

"For China?"

"Yes. He said he already has his connections and two other flyers are leaving today. That's just what he said and he wasn't talking like a crazy kid. He wasn't drunk, either. I know Paul from A to Z, and he was serious. I asked him if he wanted me to come down, and he said no, I should just talk to him."

Wilda sounded as if she had been crying.

"What did you tell him?"

"What could I tell him? I was nearly hysterical. I started to cry and laugh and yell, they probably heard me all over the office. I told him I'd drink poison if he went. I told him to come right home. Oh, I don't know what I said. But I scared him. I made him promise."

"What's the matter with him?" Jean knew well enough what was the matter with him. She was even smiling as she talked into the phone.

"I don't know, I can't figure it out. I don't know." It sounded as if Wilda was ready for another ten minutes of over-the-phone crying. Jean said she'd call later, and hung up.

When Herb came home she asked him to take her to a show after dinner. He said that there wasn't a good show in town. And anyway he couldn't get tickets now. She said she didn't care where she sat, she just felt like seeing a show.

"I'm tired."

"Please take me, Herbert."

"I'm not gonna get dressed. Look at me. I'm not gonna get dressed."

"You don't have to get dressed. You look all right."

"I feel awfully tired," he said. "I'm not even hungry."

"Come on, Herb. Just wash yourself and take me out."

He went into the bathroom and when he came out she was standing before the mirror, with that subdued orange silk underwear draped around her. Her long hair was thrown back over her shoulders, and Herb stood there, watching her.

Jean knew he was watching her, but she did not look his way. She nearly grinned into the mirror, but she tightened her face and twisted slightly. Herb came over behind her and put his fingers in her hair as it ran over her shoulders.

"What do you feel like doing now?" he said.

"I'm very hungry."

He moved away from her, and sat down on the bed, looking at her body. If ever a woman was carved out mean, it was this one. She was disastrous. And now she knew he was tired, and felt rotten, and wanted nothing but affection. Yet here she was teasing him and making him take her out for a big evening and after that she would tease him some more and it would probably end up in a fight.

But he was too tired to say anything now. He leaned back on the bed and closed his eyes. Maybe a miracle would happen and Jean would come over and kiss him.

"Should I call up Wilda? Maybe she and Paul want to come. Or should we just go alone?"

"I don't care," he said.

"I'll call up Wilda."

Call up Wilda, break a leg, drop dead, call up Wilda. He yawned and sat up on the bed. In the mirror he looked sad.

Standing there before the mirror, he stared straight-faced at himself. This was a habit of his, just standing there before the mirror and looking at himself. He did not pose. His face was expressionless. He would just stand there, staring at Herb Hervey, seeing this guy, five feet seven, 140 pounds, evenly built, with an uninteresting head of light brown hair, and green eyes, straight nose, and a growth of beard on his face that was like wire and cut like wire every time he shaved.

Jean came out of the parlor and said, "Ready?"

"I think I'll change my shirt."

"Did you take a bath?"

"No, I just washed."

"You didn't even shave?"

"No."

"Oh, go ahead and shave yourself, Herb. You look wild."

"Listen, I'm not gonna shave. See?"

They had very little to say from then on until they met Paul and Wilda Schuen at the restaurant. Wilda was always very talkative and she asked a lot of questions. So they talked a lot while they ate.

Wilda said, "Right now I'm so happy I don't know what to do. I mean that. If I could do it, I'd get up and jump on the table."

"No, don't do that," said Herb.

"Is everything all right now, Paul?" said Jean.

Paul nodded. He smiled at Jean. He was short but very heavy, and he looked like a saintly friar with a big tanned face when he smiled. He was thirty-seven. He was an engineer with an airplane manufacturing company.

"Yes," he said, "everything's all right now." He smiled at Wilda. She put her hand over his. They kept smiling at each other.

"Cut," said Herb. He put his wrists together and clapped his palms like a Hollywood director.

Paul grinned. Wilda gave Herb a dirty look. "What's the matter with him?" she said to Jean. "I thought everything was all right now."

"It is." Jean shrugged. "He's just a little tired."

Paul was always very clumsy. "Are you and Jean—all right now?"

"Sure. Come on, let's eat. It's getting late."

Jean and Wilda kept on talking. Paul looked up at Herb and then quickly looked down again. It was getting forced and unbearable but finally it was over and they were walking outside.

This was an early summer night in New York. The lights from the big street made a pink and blue glare, and the noise, the people, the cars, were brought beneath this artificial color. It rained down on them and lit them up.

A girl was soliciting funds to aid China. A man was selling razor blades. A man was looking around quickly and then quickly getting rid of dirty photographs. "Come on, hurry up, boys—six fuh two bits. Hurry up, heah comes a cop." A piano player was walking toward Fifty-second Street for a night of jam. His finger fumbled with a marijuana cigarette in his coat pocket. Another girl was soliciting funds for China.

Paul put a half-dollar in her cup. Herb said, "What's the idea?"

"Let it pass."

"No, this is good. You give four bits to aid China and then tomorrow you'll work on plans for another Japanese bomber."

"Oh, stop it, Herb," said Wilda. "Don't be small."

Herb shrugged. Paul wanted to say something but he could not get the words out. He wanted to say that Herb was right. It was a big joke. If he could have his way completely he would give up the job tomorrow. Or no, that would be too late. The boys had left today. They were on the plane already. They would get to the coast and from there they would take a boat and as soon as they reached China they would get in touch with the rest of the boys. Inside of two days they would be in the air, fighting the Japs.

So it was too late now. The boys had wanted him to come along and he wanted to go with them. What he should have done was to go and then send her a telegram as soon as he could. Instead of that he had called up. And it was the same as it had been last time, and the time before that. Now he was still in New York, and he was still with Wilda. But he still wanted to get away and fly a plane over in China.

He was thankful now that Jean and Wilda were walking on ahead. He said to Herb, "I guess Jean told you what happened today."

"No."

"Wilda stopped me from going to China."

"Again?"

"Yeah."

"You really want to go over there, don't you?"

Paul lit his fourth cigarette of the evening. He nodded.

"Why don't you go then?" said Herb.

"Wilda."

Herb frowned at him. "I don't get it. If you're so happy with her I can't see why you wanted to go in the first place. And don't give me any of this fighting-for-democracy business, either."

"No, it's not that," said Paul. "It's like a fever, I guess. You know, I haven't been doing much flying since I got the office job. And then—there's a lot of excitement over there. We get news from the boys every week."

"So you're out for thrills."

"You could call it that."

"There must be money in it, too."

"You know it's not that, Herb. I'm making good money now."

"You're better off here, then. You wouldn't make a very nice picture with ten or fifteen machine-gun bullets plastered in your head."

"But this way, I don't know, it's not that I'm neurotic—or—but every goddamn day, getting up, running to the office, bending over a desk, figures, scales, slide rules, specifications, you go nuts. Especially when you've been in the air, you've been flying ever since you were twenty, it gets you. I don't know, it's hard to explain. But I just have that feeling—I want the excitement."

It was hard to figure, a settled boy like Paul talking this way. Wilda was no angel, but you didn't have to look twice to see that she was crazy about Paul. Herb thought how lucky some guys were, all they had to do was exist and be loved. Paul never had to act, he never had to force words out of his mouth. All he had to do was be around, and if Wilda was there with him, he would be loved. At least, it looked that way from the outside. Herb looked at her, walking in front with Jean. Wilda wasn't doing bad.

They had rotten seats for the show, and he was sick of shows anyway. They were getting away with murder, some of this stuff he had seen recently. Ability and talent, real quality, were smothered up by a lot of big shots and publicity and general all-around crap. Well, it was that way in everything. Or maybe it was because he felt so low and disgusted and hating-the-world. One of the actors missed a line and Herb felt better.

Near the end of the second act Jean hissed, "Please sit still."

He hadn't known he was moving around so much. "Sorry," he said. This was really getting bad. He remembered when he was a kid, and on Saturday matinees they gave free apples. You threw apples at one another and sometimes you threw them at the villain. Once he had done that. He had been kicked out.

Right now he wanted to do something like that. If he had an apple or better still a tomato he would like to pitch it at one of those punks on the stage. Then an usher would come and kick him out. Oh, yeah? They'd need more than one punk of an usher to kick him out. They'd need six. What was wrong? He had not taken a shot of liquor all day. All right, try to get your mind on the stage.

"Oh, Herbert, please!"

"Aw, what's wrong?"

"Sh-sh—sit still."

Paul was sitting between Jean and Wilda. Wilda put her hand down and touched Paul's arm. He straightened his arm and clasped her hand. They sat this way for a while. Then Paul put his arm on the side of the chair and Wilda took her hand away. Jean put her hand down and Paul touched her arm. She looked sideways for an instant and Paul glanced at her. They both smiled slightly.

"That wasn't so bad," said Paul. They were getting into his Chrysler.

"The last act was the best."

"What makes you say that, Jean?"

"I don't know, it seemed so—sincere."

Herb wanted to laugh. She was a good one to talk about sincerity.

"Let's go somewhere," said Paul.

"You're driving, Paul."

"That's all right," said Herb. "We can have a few drinks."

"Oh, we don't have to go anywhere. We can have a few over at our place."

"I'd rather not." Wilda was using that whining, nagging tone that sounds like an old record with a much-used needle.

"Come on, dear," said Paul. "We'll celebrate my—staying home."

"I don't see where we need to celebrate anything like that," said

Wilda. "In fact—oh, skip it."

Paul drove them home and not much was said. They got off and Wilda said, "I'll call you, Jean."

In the elevator Jean murmured, "They're going to fight."

"I'm worried," said Herb.

"Are you still tired?"

"Not so much now."

"I'm not tired either."

"Well?"

"So we don't have to go to bed yet," she said.

They were at the third floor. As they moved slowly through the hall he said, "Did you hear me mention anything about going to bed?"

She did not answer him. He dropped into a chair and began reading the *Telegraph*. Jean turned on the radio. A swing band was blaring.

"Do we need that?" said Herb.

She snapped it off. She stood there looking at him. He put the paper down. He gave her look for look. She began to breathe hard. He got up. She took a step toward him.

"What do you want to do?" He wondered whether to laugh at her.

"At least one of us is trying to put things right," she said softly. She surprised him with that one. He let it sink in.

"All right. I know that. But what do you want me to do?"

She did not answer. She looked at him. It was just this matter of standing there and looking at him and he couldn't tell whether she wanted to put a knife in him or press her lips against his.

This had been going on and off for three years. Sometimes he would get together with himself, and try to add two and two. But he would never get four.

"Sit down. Let's talk," he said.

"I don't feel like talking."

If she would smile saying that, or move toward him, or do something, then all right. But to stand there and say something and just stand there, it was too much for him. If this was what she had come back for, then she might just as well be in Africa.

"What do you feel like doing?" He took a step toward her. He did not wait for her to answer. As if she was a halfback who had just taken a kickoff, and he was an end racing down the field, he went for her. He got her around the waist and the two of them fell over a chair. She grabbed his hair and began to pull. It hurt and tears rushed from his eyes. He had to let go of her before she pulled his hair out.

Then he was sitting there like a dope and she was sitting beside him, breathing heavily. He shook his head and Jean looked at his face.

"You're—crying. I hurt you," she said. She got up on her knees and put her arms around him, forced him down on the floor. Then she slowly lowered her head and moved her lips around on his, pressing them down, and pressing herself down against him. This went on. She unbuttoned his shirt and put her hands against his stomach and then against his sides. He pulled her up hard against him. They were kissing and he finally picked her up and carried her into the bedroom. He was a small man but he was steel, and she could feel his arms hard against her. She could hear and feel him getting excited, and then when he put her down on the bed she saw that he was in a bad state.

"Wait, Herb."

"Wait? What for, a trolley car?"

"Please, Herb, please. Please wait."

"Why?"

"I don't want to."

"Why?"

"I just don't want to—all of a sudden."

"Don't you feel good?"

"Don't I—? Oh—no. No, I don't feel good."

"You're lying, Jean. Don't lie. For once, for this once, tell me what's wrong. I'm begging you, Jean, tell me what's wrong."

"I—"

"Jean, I want you to get this right. Ever since I first met you we've had trouble with each other. I don't know what it is, but I know this much. It's not my fault. I don't want it broken up. You—I—I don't see how I could keep on going without you. But then it's the same thing when I'm with you. I—" He was nearly crying. It was tough not to cry. Herb was digging down into his soul and throwing it out of himself. "Don't drive me crazy, Jean. For Christ's sake, leave me alone and don't drive me crazy."

"Why are you blaming me?" She was looking at him curiously, as if he was on exhibit.

"You want to keep on living with me. You want to keep on being my wife. You—" He threw his hands down, unable to say more. His throat was choked up, he hurried out of the room. No sooner was he out than she slammed the door shut and locked it.

Herb turned around and saw the closed door. He opened his mouth slowly until there was a big wide grin on his face. Then he nodded. So Jean was in there now and she expected him to beg. She was in there having some crazy revenge and she pictured him tortured to death looking at that closed door.

He came up close to the door. "Good night, bitch," he said, and rushed out of the apartment, into the street. He walked fast, and a taxi passed. He waved his arm. The cab stopped for him.

Jean bit into the pillow. Her teeth gnawed at the cotton. She wanted Paul. He was sleeping with Wilda and she wanted him to get out of Wilda's bed and come over here. Please, Paul, she said to the pillow, please come over here. Why didn't you leave today, Paul? Please, why didn't you leave? Herb, Herb, come back then. Paul isn't coming over. I know he isn't. So you come back, Herb. Oh, no, stay away, stay away. Where did you go, you crazy Herb? Where did you go? Oh, Paul.

If he went to the docks he might be able to sneak aboard a ship. Then matters would be completely out of his hands. Perhaps that wouldn't be so sweet either. In case he wanted to change his mind later it would be too late. Funny how yellow he was at times. When was the last time he had been in a fight? Years ago. And then it had not been much of a scrap. He could stand a little excitement. But he didn't want to get hurt. Somehow he felt that he did not want any trouble, any pain. He felt very yellow.

"All right. I'll get out here."

"Here?" said the taxi driver.

He got out. This was Harlem. It was a little past midnight. He walked slowly, looking at his shoes, then at his trousers. He buttoned his shirt but he didn't have a tie on.

A lot of noise came from a place on the corner. Outside the Negroes were laughing and yelling. Herb passed by. A big black girl started to follow him. He turned the corner and she hissed.

He shook his head. She went back around the corner.

There was a small side street facing him now and he stood there for a moment deciding. A couple of the boys might jump on him and razor his throat. He pictured a couple big dark boys jumping on him and cutting him up. He shrugged and entered the street.

It was very dark and only a few of the tenements were lit up. From one of these someone was coming out onto the street and then turning off in front of him. It was a girl. She was walking fast and he started to follow her. She turned and saw him and kept on walking the same way, not faster, not slower.

This girl was built something terrific. She did not have much on and Herb wanted to see what her plans were. He came up close behind her and whistled. She turned around and shook her head.

If she was a Negro she was very light. She did not look as if she had Negro blood in her. Staring at her more closely he did not have any doubts. She was probably Italian. He walked beside her.

"No," she said, "try another street." She talked as if she was giving him directions, and he was a lost boy.

He could see her very plainly now. She had black gleaming hair and a face that was perfectly balanced. She had no paint on and she looked very sweet.

Now she was turning around but he said, "Wait, just a—look, where you going?"

"I can't help you out. There's plenty of girls on other streets."

"Maybe you got the wrong idea."

"Oh. Well then, what do you want? If you're a thief you won't find any money on me. And if you're a detective you can't arrest me, because I haven't done anything." She seemed amused. She didn't appear to be in any particular hurry.

"No, I'm not a crook and I'm not a cop. I'm just a plain guy and I want somebody to talk to. I got a bad case of the blues. I just ran away from my wife."

"Why did you do that?" They were walking slowly down the street together.

"She locked the door on me. That's reason enough, isn't it?"

"Oh, I don't think so. You should have broken down the door." It was a curious thing. She had a very cultured voice. She did not smell of perfume and yet she smelled very sweet. It was a delight to walk beside her.

"No, I wouldn't do that. I wouldn't do anything like that. I just got so sad and disgusted that I ran out of the place and took a cab. I don't know why I came up here."

"Maybe you better go back and she'll open up the door for you."

"No. She won't do that. I know her."

"Well, if I were you I wouldn't walk down side streets like this. You might get in trouble if you don't know the neighborhood."

"Do you live here, on this street?"

"No," she said. "I live two blocks away. I was visiting a friend."

"Can I walk you home?"

"Of course."

"Why did you say I might get in trouble?"

"Oh, things are very bad up here now. There are fights, and the women are bad, and then there's so little money, they'll do almost anything for—"

"Yeah, these niggers—" He knew he shouldn't have said that.

"Please don't say that."

"Oh, I'm sorry, I didn't know you were—"

"No, I'm not colored, and I have no special love for my immediate neighbors up here. But I don't like that word. It carries too much of hate. I detest hate, particularly when there's no logical reason for it."

"That's a nice way of looking at things, but it's pretty hard to follow."

"Yes, it is hard to follow. That's what makes tolerance such a fine ideal. I have an excuse to hate, I have many excuses, and the biggest problem in my life is to put that hate aside."

Herb wanted to look at her while she was speaking, but every word she said made him concentrate more on what she was saying rather than on what she looked like. They were standing now in front of a miserable tenement from which no light came.

"I live here," she said. "I only have one room. If you have no place to stay you're welcome to come up and sleep. I can make room for you."

"What about your family?"

"I have no family. My husband—is in Spain." She was walking up the steps. Herb followed her. On the second-floor landing she turned to the left and motioned him to be careful not to trip. It was very dark.

The room was small. There was a bed, a chair, a bureau, a mirror, a washstand. It was all very clean. It seemed to become even cleaner as she walked in. She put on the light and then he really saw her.

There was no use trying to say anything. He looked at her and he couldn't do a thing. He stood there and looked at that face and she said, "I'm sorry I can't offer you anything to eat. You see, I take my meals over at my friend's room. That was where I just came from."

"You live here all alone then." He sat down on the chair and she was resting on the bed. She flipped off her shoes.

"Yes. I could stay over there but they're awfully crowded, and I make enough to pay the rent here."

"Oh, you work."

"Yes, I do piece work in a shirt factory. I make enough to pay rent and pay for my meals, and—oh, I get along."

"You said your husband was in Spain?"

"Yes." Her voice was lowered.

"Fighting?"

She nodded. Her head was slightly lowered.

"Is he Spanish?"

She shook her head. "No, he's Italian."

"Well, you're Italian too, aren't you?"

She smiled. "No."

"How come?"

"How come what?"

"Spain."

"Oh, that's a long story. But my husband was one of the first volunteers to join up."

"He must be pretty young."

"What makes you say that?"

"Oh, most of these boys that went over there. You know, young, they want a thrill. I got a friend who wants to go to—"

"Wait. Wait a minute. I'm afraid you don't understand." Her voice was very soft, and very kind, yet he had a feeling that what she was about to say would make him feel like two cents. "You see," she began, "my husband did not go over there for a thrill. My husband is an exile from Italy. He's fighting with the Garibaldi Legion. That's part of the International Brigade. And those men are not in Spain for thrills and adventure."

"Well, I didn't exactly mean—"

"You see, my husband's father was murdered in Italy because he was a pacifist and an anti-Fascist. And now Tommy is fighting for those ideals."

Herb nodded. He did not know enough about this Spanish business either to argue or agree with her. All he knew was that there was a war going on over there and they were killing each other and every once in a while a few bombs would be dropped on a city, or there would be a big advance or a little trouble with France or England or Italy or Germany or Russia. It was a big mess and sometimes it made interesting reading in the papers when he had nothing else to do.

"I guess—you miss him." Gee, he thought, what a dope I am.

She got up. "Look, I'll show you some pictures." From a bureau drawer she took a few photographs and Herb saw this Tommy. He was a good-looking guy about thirty years old. He looked strong and hard as rock. And he looked clean. There was something right about him.

"Before he went away he worked for a builder. He had a good job. But he was always giving money to some cause. I had a lot of trouble with the rascal. Some weeks he wanted to give every cent he had. Oh, we had some fine fights on account of that. Didn't we, didn't we, you—you—" she put the picture to her mouth and kissed it.

Dorothy took out another picture. It was from a magazine circulated among members of the International Brigade. It showed Tommy in the trenches. He was ready for an offensive.

"That was taken just before he was wounded. I got a letter from him with this. They took this picture and then they attacked. And he was wounded." Her voice quivered slightly. She seemed to feel the pain all over again.

"Well, then he's not fighting now?"

"He's still fighting," she said. "Almost as soon as he got out of the hospital he went back into the trenches."

Her voice was quivering now, and he knew she did not want to talk about it anymore. They were silent in this room and he wanted to go out. He wanted to get out in a hurry and yet he knew that if he went out he would want to come back. He kept looking at her now as she put the pictures away and at last he forced himself to take his eyes off her.

"Maybe I better go now," he said, and it sounded foolish.

"No, stay here." Dorothy was looking at him steadily.

"You want me to stay here."

"Yes."

"Why?"

"It will be better for you." She sounded like a nurse.

"Then—"

"You're all right," she said. "You look perfectly all right to me."

"What does that mean?"

She was not smiling. She breathed earnestly and there was a slight frown between her eyes and she said, "You can stay here."

Herb waited awhile. Before he said anything else he wanted to get this straight in his mind. One thing he already knew. This Dorothy represented a class of human being a few million degrees above parasites like himself and Jean and the rest of the crowd. Already he felt slightly choked in her presence.

"It's late," she was saying now. "I have to get up early. Excuse me a minute." She went out of the room. He heard her in the hallway.

In a few minutes she came back. She laughed. "We're lucky. We have a bathroom on the same floor. If you have to go it's just two doors down."

Then he sat down on the bed. He was limp. Words were coming up to his lips and he wanted to stop them then and there. But they were rushing out and he was saying, "Please don't stand in front of me like that. I don't want to look at you. You're the most beautiful— you're—I've never seen anything quite like you before. Don't—I shouldn't be here. But—"

She came over and put her hand on his mouth. "It's really very late. We ought to get some rest."

Then he was taking off his clothes and he was going into the bathroom. When he came into Dorothy's room again the light was out but he could see her on the bed. There was a smooth breeze coming into the room and there was a moon in the center of the window frame. The room was dark blue and there was this silver light hitting the mirror and the metal edge of the bed and this soft glow of silver blue on Dorothy as she rested there on one side. So now he was placing himself on the other side of the bed, then lying down, and waiting for her to say something. But she did not even murmur good night. Already she was breathing the deep steady rhythm of a tired body that needs rest.

Right now he decided that he was either going to leave her alone or get out of the room. All right, Herb, he told himself, you're going to leave her alone, do you understand? You're going to leave her alone. Now go to sleep and forget about her.

The breeze came in and made a steady *whirrr* against the windowpane. Dorothy was breathing more deeply. And then Herb was very tired. And he turned over to close his eyes and suddenly fell asleep.

Hours later something was opening his eyes, bringing him to his senses. Someone was talking. He wondered where he was. He heard this soft voice whispering, "Where are you now, my dear lover? What are they doing to you? Are you in the trenches now? Have you been fighting? You're tired, you're bleeding, oh, Tommy, I know, I know you're hurt again. Tommy, lover, please—when will you come back to me? How long must I wait for you? How long must I be alone without you? Please, dear one, come back, won't you please come back? I really need you so much—really I—" She put her arm out and turned over. As she did this he felt her hand across his forehead. For an instant he had the impulse to run away.

She moved toward him and he could see her eyes closed. "Tommy," she whispered, "lover, I can feel you near me."

He edged away from her and nearly fell on the floor. He heard her murmuring as he got dressed and then he quietly moved around to the door, opened it, and left.

It was thick and hot in the early yellow-gray morning. There was no breeze now and it was going to be a sticky day. In the subway Herb kept thinking how tough this day was going to be on the workers in the factories, and he was still thinking about this as he entered the apartment.

CHAPTER II

On the drafting table before Paul there were all these plans and drawing instruments. His head was going around like the propeller on the tri-motored job he was figuring out here. Then the telephone had to ring and he had to answer it.

It was Jean. He wanted to hang up. But she was talking fast and he could picture her sitting there yelling into the phone. She was saying, "Whatever you're doing, I don't care what you're doing now, I've got to see you. I swear, Paul, if you don't come right over I'm going to cut my throat. I mean it, I swear I'll cut my throat if you don't come over now. I'm going crazy, I can feel myself going crazy and I don't—" That kept up for more than a minute and she was getting on his nerves, because it wasn't the first time Jean had carried on like this.

"Tell me what's wrong with you. Was there a fight?"

"I've got to see you, Paul. Please."

He shook his head slowly, teeth together, and got off the high stool. He told his secretary he would be back soon and then he left the office.

In the apartment Jean was lying face down on the sofa and he knew that this was a carefully worked-out pose. She had it down pat, all right. Her shoulders were heaving without undue exaggeration and she gave the impression of multiplied misery. Maybe she really was badly off, he figured. He stood there waiting for her to come out of it.

Jean raised her head and sobbed, "Oh, Paul—" and then went down again, and cried harder.

He looked at it this way. She probably did not feel any too happy, but it wasn't this bad. It couldn't be this bad.

Well, now he was expected to sit down beside her and pat her head and then begin kissing her and asking what was wrong, and then telling her that everything would be all right.

Jean raised her head. She had the kind of face which looks nicest when there is paint on it. She did not look so good now. Paul waited for her to say something and she cried, "Paul, let's go away!"

"Oh, cut it out. Listen, Jean, you can't keep on doing this. It's bad, you know it's bad as well as I do."

"I can't help it."

"What did he do?"

"He wanted to kill me last night. I had to lock the door. Then he went out. I don't know where he went. I was wishing he'd go jump off a bridge. But then he came back early in the morning. He didn't ask me to unlock the door. He didn't even say anything. Not a word. I think he took a shower and then made himself a cup of coffee but he didn't say one word."

"Here I thought everything was going to be all right."

"It'll never be all right. I can't stand him."

"You've told me that before, but you've never given me a good reason. Now listen, Jean, you'll have to do something. I'm not blaming—"

"Shut up—shut up, shut up, it's your fault. It's all your fault. Please take me away with you, Paul. Let's go away. You know you love me. Paul—"

"Don't, Jean."

"But you love me. You love me. You do, don't you?"

"Yes." At the same time he was telling himself that this was a joke. It was mean, it was rotten, it hurt him inside, and the whole thing was just too bad. But here it was, and she was not having fun with him, she was really sick over him. It had been going on this way for nearly a year, and it was getting worse all the time. Yet it was a joke. If he was watching this, if he was up there hidden in the ceiling, watching something like this go on, he would laugh.

"I don't want to cry, Paul," she was saying. "And I didn't want to bring you here like this. I'm so sorry. But I couldn't help it. I couldn't help it all the other times and it was the same way this time. It will be the same way next time. I don't know what to do, Paul. Paul—"

"What, Jean?"

"Can you get a divorce?"

"I don't want a divorce."

"You've got to let Wilda go, Paul. And I can't live with Herb any longer. That's all. That's final. It's the only thing we can do."

"I'm not getting a divorce."

"But you love me."

"That's something over which I have no control, Jean. It's gotten so that I'm willing to love you and not see you."

"Then go away. Go away now." She started to cry again. "Go to China, go to Asia, go to hell—" she threw herself down again on the sofa and he stood up. He bit his lip and started slowly toward the door. Then he turned back and came over to Jean again. He sat down beside her and lifted her in his arms. But even though she tried to get him close he would not kiss her.

"Maybe I will go away, Jean. I don't know. We'll see how things work out. In the meantime try and look at things sensibly. I'm married to Wilda. And you're married to Herb. Let's not act like a couple of rats. We've done plenty already. Now let's try and be good for a while."

"Sometimes you're a clown, Paul."

"All right, I'm a clown. But from the mouths of fools—you've heard that one. I'm only trying to be decent for a change, Jean."

She shook her head, and said nothing. He got up. "All right now?"

"No."

Paul shrugged. "You'll be all right." He went out.

For an hour afterward she stayed on the sofa, just resting on her stomach and looking at the white rug. Then she got up and took a cold shower. Only when the water was running over her head did she realize how hot and uncomfortable she had been. She got dressed and took a taxi into town.

A few things happened to her when she dropped into one of the smart hotels for a tall iced drink. She was sitting at a gleaming bronze table in a bronze room with green mirrors and a green ceiling, and a young man came in and sat down at the same table. She looked at him curiously, and he was staring straight at her.

"Do you mind if I sit here?" he said.

"Why—no." But there were other empty tables and he was probably a wise guy. He looked young. He was about five ten and he was built heavily. He had a very short crew haircut, and his face was square and slightly tan beneath the blonde hair.

"I'm awfully lonesome," he said. "I must talk to someone. I've been looking for a job and I can't get one. Really, I'm very low." He stopped to order a gin rickey.

"Go on," she said. "You were very low."

"Oh. Yeah. Well, I am. Maybe you know some place where I could get a job."

"Maybe. What do you do?"

"Just graduated Princeton. Law. Age twenty-seven. That's because I played two years of prep football after I got out of high school. Then I played football at North Carolina after I made All-New Jersey scholastic at guard. I was a whiz. Look at me now."

"I'm looking."

"How am I?"

"Not too bad."

"My name's George Green. Isn't that a shame? A name like that?"

"You can always put an initial before it. E. George Green would sound better."

"Say, that's an idea. E. George Green. And how about you?"

"Jean Hervey." She was looking him over rather closely now. He was wearing a dark blue tropical with a pinstripe. He had a white loosely woven shirt with a dark blue knitted tie. There was a thick gold safety pin in his collar. She imagined that he wore thick-soled cordovan shoes.

"You're probably an actress."

"I'm probably not."

"Then you're a model."

"No."

"You ought to be one."

"Think so?"

"Look, do you know anyone who could help me out?"

She laughed. "You're being very silly. I think you're kidding. Stop it."

"No, I'm not," said George. "I really do need a job bad. Oh, I have a little money, but that's not the point. I want something to do."

"Why don't you collect string?"

"Why don't you have dinner with me this evening?"

That night she had dinner with him. Herb came home from the office and found a note to the effect that she was spending the night at a friend's place in the country. He put the note down where he had found it and went over to his garage. He took a long drive and came back early and went to bed.

In the morning he woke up surprised that he had slept so well. He had a good day at the office and at five o'clock he called up to tell her that he would not be home. But no one answered the phone. He ate in town with a friend and then came back to the apartment. She was still out. The note was still where he had left it. He called up the Schuens.

Wilda said that she had not heard from Jean.

It's okay, he told himself. It's perfectly okay with me. And he wasn't just forcing those words into himself. He really felt that way.

CHAPTER III

No one answered the bell. Herb tried the door. It was open and he went up to the second floor. Her room was empty. The whole house seemed empty. He wondered where her friend lived. She was probably still over there. He left the tenement and then he saw her walking up the street toward him.

At sight of her he wanted to run and jump and yell how glad he was to see her. She came up to him and said, "Hello."

She was really glad to see him. She did not seem to notice the change in his appearance, although he was wearing a new summer suit and new shoes and a good-looking blue shirt.

"I'm sorry about the other day. I never thanked you."

"You left pretty early," she said.

"Just coming back from your friend's?"

"Yes. Tonight I have to work."

"Work? You have to work extra hours?"

"Oh, no. This work is for Spain. I'm soliciting aid. Suppose I begin with you. Do you have any change on you? Or maybe you—"

He put his hand in his pocket and took out a roll of bills. "Will twenty be enough to start?"

"You can afford that?"

"Just about."

"Thank you very much." She put the money in a pocket. "Where do you work?"

"Well, tonight I'll go around the Bronx. That's an easy territory. A lot of sympathizers there."

"How do you go about this work?"

"It's not hard. Door to door. I carry literature with me and also a big bag, in case they want to donate canned goods or books or cigarettes. On Sundays sometimes we get a horse and wagon. Tonight I'm going alone, because my friend doesn't feel very well."

"Can't I take you? That's my car." He pointed.

"Oh. Well, it would be very nice of you."

They were in his convertible green Pontiac and he was driving toward the Bronx.

"How do things look over there, Dorothy?"

"It's bad, like the papers say. But you never can tell. I don't know much about the military situation, but if you look at one of the maps you can see that they're being pushed back. If they could only gain time and then strike back, just get a few of those important points and hold them, and then bolster their defense, it would perhaps mean everything. But now—it does look very bad."

"But they're still fighting."

"They'll always fight. They'll never give up." She was not talking like a cheerleader. She was only saying something which she felt to be true. He could not detect a single note of artificiality in anything she said.

"You have plenty of room in this car, don't you?"

"Yes. Why don't you call me Herb?"

"I didn't know that was your name, Herb. Look, Herb, would it be all right to put the things in the back, and then you'd drive down to the center so I could give it to them down there?"

"You must expect a lot of donations."

"Oh, yes. People are kind about these things."

They filled up the entire rear of the car. She would go from door to door and he would ride slowly down the block, and every time there were gifts of canned goods or magazines, he would run up and take them down to the car. They worked until eleven o'clock. He drove down to Greenwich Village and Dorothy handed in the money and the goods.

"I made you drive around too much," she said.

"Let's really take a ride now. Let's get out of the city. I'll tell you what. Let's really take a long ride. Then we'll be real hungry and tired and we can stay some place overnight."

"Yes, but we'll have to get up real early tomorrow so you can take me to the factory."

"You won't go to the factory tomorrow. Quit your job there. I'll get you a better job."

"How can you do that?"

"We can make an opening in my office. That is, where I work."

"No, Herb, I don't want you to do that," she said. "You're going to fire one of the other girls, aren't you?"

"No, I—"

"That's what you would do. I don't want you to do that."

They drove out into the country. The night was very warm and even though the car zipped along at sixty the wind did not cool them. They leaned back and drove along and finally turned in at a narrow road.

"Where are we now?"

"I don't know."

"Let's stop," she said.

"Isn't it hot?"

"I wish there was a lake or a pool."

"Can you swim?" said Herb.

"Oh, I can swim swell. How about you?"

"I can keep up. I can swim as well as any woman."

"Oh, yeah? We'll see. Let's keep driving until we find a place, and then we'll see. A smart guy."

He put the car in reverse and backed out of the road. They kept on going and it was all black and dark green around them until the dark green was broken off by something silver shining through the trees.

"Oh, look, Herb—"

He parked and they went over. They had to walk about fifty yards through the woods until they came to the spot. It was a pond. It looked too perfect to be a natural pond. And there were large stones fringing it in almost a perfect circle. They looked down at the water and Dorothy bent on her hands and knees and took some to her face.

"Mmmm—just right."

"Well, it's hot and the water's cool, and I feel like swimming."

"Do you want to know something?"

"I think I know what you're going to say. I suspect the same thing. We're on private property."

"We'll be arrested," she said. She laughed.

"Oh, well, they can't hang us."

"I'm afraid. I'm a sissy." She laughed.

"Come on."

"You go in first."

He took off all his clothes and jumped in. "Wheeee—ooohh, it's cold! Boy, it's really cold. But it's swell. Come on in, it's really grand.

You're coming in, aren't you? No kidding, it's swell!" He swam about spluttering while Dorothy undressed.

"Come on, slowpoke!"

"Here I come, ready or not—" she took a running jump and landed with a splash near him. She came up laughing and trying to duck him. She pushed his head under and then he grabbed her and they went under together. It was deep and they came up fast as soon as their feet failed to touch bottom.

"Say, it's really deep," she said.

"Let's swim over there. It may be shallow at that end." They could stand over at the opposite side. They splashed about and then she said, "Race?"

"Aw, it'll be too easy."

She splashed him. "Come on."

They got out and then she yelled, "Ready, set, go!" They dove. Almost as soon as they came up there was the sound of someone running toward them. They turned fast and swam toward the edge. They picked up their clothes.

"Oh, boy—"

"Legs, do yo' stuff," she said. He started to laugh. They were running naked toward the car. Someone was trying to find them with a flashlight.

"Hey, you two! Stop where you are!"

"Ouch," said Dorothy.

"Come on, come on," he gasped. "We'll look at it in the car."

"Oh, it's nothing. Just a broken leg, I guess," and she raced ahead of him. They got to the car and he got started just as someone broke out of the woods and yelled for them to stop. There was a turn in the road and Herb made it before the flashlight could focus steadily on his license number.

"Hurry, Jim," she said, "only five more miles to the border."

"Right, pardner, giddyap, pinto ol' boy."

"Say, I really did hurt my foot, you know that? Ouch. I don't know what it was I stepped on."

"We'll stop and look at it. Oh, wait a minute. There's a signpost. I want to see where we are." He drew up alongside the post and then he said, "There's cabins near here. We can spend the night. There's a regular camp there."

"We'll both have colds in the morning. It's all your fault."

"If you squeal to Ma I'll punch you right in the teeth, you get me?"

They managed to cover themselves with the clothes as they got up to the cabins. Herb paid the keeper and they went in and dried themselves and then dressed. The clothes were damp and uncomfortable but it was all right because they were laughing and wisecracking. She had only turned her ankle and every time it hurt she winced and giggled. They went over to one of the stands around the camp and had a lot to eat. Then they walked along toward the cabin, smoking.

When they drew up the flaps to let air in, and a sudden coolness hit them, Dorothy turned to him and said, "It's nice and cool here now, isn't it?"

"Yes. What's the matter?"

"It must be awfully hot over in—"

She sat down on the bed, facing away from him. He came over and put his hand on her shoulder.

"What's the matter, Dorothy?"

She shook her head and then slowly she bent over and put her face in the pillow. He could see that she was trying to get a grip on herself, but it broke all of a sudden and she was sobbing quietly. Pain after pain ran through him as he stood there, and he just couldn't say anything.

He couldn't do anything more except put the light out and lie down on the other small bed. Slowly her sobs were dying down and finally she fell asleep.

In the early morning she was joking and laughing again as they drove through the wet green countryside toward the city. Herb left her off at the factory and said that he would be up to see her tonight. He sat there looking at her as she entered the factory.

Sometimes a guy gets filled with a heavy sadness that is suddenly covered over by a grin and a laugh. And then over that there comes another sadness, something fine and beautiful that can't be explained. It just exists there. And over this there comes another grin and another laugh. Sometimes it just keeps up this way. There is this pain, and then there is this laugh. And above it all there is a big question mark.

CHAPTER IV

Most of the guys in the office were jerks. He never had much to do with them. At times he figured that it was as much his fault as theirs. But they impressed him very little. He saw enough of them eight hours a day to know he was missing very little by cultivating their friendship.

They were all smug and snobbish. He had always held that impression, but not until today had it occurred to him how low they were. They were all college graduates. There were a few Columbia men, like himself, and then Pennsylvania, Cornell, and one or two other big schools, besides a few of the Midwestern colleges, had sent their shave-once-a-day boys to this big advertising agency, and now they made good money and acted big and wore draped double-breasted suits and starched collars and smelled of whisky after lunch hour.

And not until this very minute, sitting here and thinking the whole thing over, had it occurred to Herb what a jerk he himself was. He was really no better than the rest of the boys. He was one of them and as a unit they represented very little of anything truly important.

Make good money every week by not working too hard for it and then the ads appear in the magazines and over the radio and door-to-door and then the suckers go out and get chiseled, and the money comes rolling in. The four bits goes sliding across the bar and the Scotch goes down. The tailor measures out another suit. Another car is taken out of the factory and delivered, the milliner sends another bill, the big shop on Fifth Avenue sends another bill, eight hours a day, sitting and figuring out new ways to get dough, get dough, and then go home and figure ways to save it, ways to spend it, ways to have a good time.

What is a good time? What constitutes enjoyment? He sat there, leaning back and biting into a soft-lead pencil. One of the girls came in and gave him a few sheets of paper containing writing and figures and diagrams. He put the papers down and looked at his wristwatch. Five more minutes until twelve o'clock. He got up and went into the next office.

"Miss Gillen."

"Yes, Mr. Hervey."

"Those papers you just brought into my office—" The other girls, a few of the men were looking at him already. He shrugged. "Would you please step into my office, Miss Gillen?"

She shook her head slightly and sighed resignedly. She got up and followed him into his office.

"Look, these papers," he said. "You know what's to be done with them, don't you?"

"No."

"You're lying."

"I got my own work to do, Mr. Hervey."

"That's all right. You take care of those papers for me and I'll treat you nicely."

"What do you—"

"Go on, take the papers. I want to go to the ballgame this afternoon. You finish them up for me and I'll give you five bucks for the afternoon's work."

"But really, Mr. Hervey—" She was frightened, as if he was trying to bite her. This had never happened before.

"How much do you get a week, Miss Gillen?"

"Why—twenty-five."

"All right. Take a little off my hands once or twice a week and I'll give you an extra five. How's that?"

"No. I can't see myself doing that. I'm sorry, Mr. Hervey. It wouldn't be honest."

"You're crazy. Any other girl in the office would be only too glad."

"It's cheating."

"What are you, a Campfire Girl or something? If I wanted to be mean, I could order you to do those papers."

"You could not." She straightened up and looked him right in the eye. He wondered if she had a boyfriend. She wasn't so bad.

"So I couldn't, is that it? Suppose I casually sent down a note to Mr. Edwinns saying that you showed signs of falling down on the job, and that I was dissatisfied with your work?"

"You—you wouldn't do a thing like that."

"No. But I could if I wanted to. I'm giving you a break. Don't be a stooge to Edwinns or anybody else around here."

"Including yourself."

"You won't be stooging, stupid. I'll be paying you, but the whole world doesn't have to know."

She inclined her head slightly to think it over. He bent toward her a little. She really wasn't so bad. For the first time he noticed that she was built high. She was studying him and he grinned at her. She grinned back. He put out his hands and she took them and he pulled her over to him and said, "I got a lot on my mind these days and I want to take it easy. You be nice to me and we'll get along."

"Financially," she said.

He nodded. He gave her a five-dollar bill. "If anyone asks where I went, say I had a couple of appointments, will you?"

She nodded. He was going to put his hand on her, but suddenly something held it back and she was looking at him oddly and he realized that he must have a funny look on his face right now. He motioned for her to go out and then he was settling slowly in his chair.

This was all very dumb. It was so dumb that it was a panic. He didn't want to go to the ballgame now. He wanted to do those papers himself. So he had gone and thrown five bucks to the winds. There was a dame in the office outside who had been working here before he had come on, four years ago. And all this time they hadn't said boo to one another outside of what was strictly business. Now she had him down for a screwball. He felt very dumb.

Someone came into the office and it was this Miss Gillen. She said, "You're doing the papers yourself?"

"Yes."

"Then here's the five—"

"No. Keep that. It's a present. You're a good worker. And you don't talk too much."

"Thanks, Mr. Hervey." She was giving him a fairly agreeable glance. "If I can do anything any time—"

"Oh, sure, Miss Gillen, I guess you can do something for me sometime." He smiled back agreeably. "And now if you don't mind, I'll start on these papers."

After he was well started on the papers there was a click in his brain and he began thinking in practical terms about this Miss Gillen. He needed something like that. He wondered what had held him back just before. Then there was another click in his mind and he was thinking of Jean. But that didn't last long. The third click nearly knocked him to the floor. He tried to shake it off, he stared at one spot on the floor for fifteen minutes, but it wouldn't go away. He kept trying and he even forced himself to think about different things like what Gomez would do today against Cleveland, and how his Armour stock was going, and whether he should buy himself a new wristwatch. But it was no use. It kept on. It was there in front of him just like the floor, the window, his desk. He saw Dorothy in front of him and she wouldn't go away. She was there, she wasn't smiling at him, she wasn't doing anything. She was just there. He saw her. He kept staring at her and all the while he was saying to himself, I mustn't let this happen to me, I mustn't let this happen.

Through that entire day he saw her. He did not finish the papers, he did not eat lunch. He went back to the apartment with a bad headache and a dull throbbing deep inside.

Jean was reading a magazine. She looked cool and comfortable. The blinds were up and the room, orange and white, took some of the heat away. Next to the chair on which Jean was sitting there was a pitcher of lemonade.

"It's good to see you again," he said. "I missed you."

"Yeah. Any more jokes?"

"Where've you been keeping yourself?"

"Does it make any difference?"

"No." He looked at her as if she was made of stone. "You don't look well at all, do you know that?"

"I don't feel very well," he said. "That lemonade looks cold."

"Take some."

He poured himself a glass and then he said, "Who is it this time?"

Jean wouldn't answer. Herb went into the bathroom and took a shower. But that didn't make him feel any better. He still had this bad headache. He could hear the phone ringing while he was drying himself. He could hear Jean talking to someone. He heard her say, "All right, eight will be all right. Make it about a quarter after eight."

Herb dressed slowly and while he was putting on his tie Jean came into the room. She started to fix her hair in front of the mirror and he saw that she was trying to attract his attention. She started to twist her hips slightly and he bounded over to her and gave her a push. She went against the door and he gave her another push and she tripped hard and fell in the hallway. He slammed the door shut and she called him a few names while she was still sitting down. Her voice sounded harsh and ugly coming from the hallway.

Already he began to feel a little better. There was a satisfying feeling coming into the pit of his stomach and moving out toward his back. He went into the bathroom and soon he did not have the headache or the heavy dull throbbing. He put cold water on his face and looked in the mirror. Now he really felt good and he was very hungry. Jean was in the bedroom again and the door was locked. His suit coat was in there and he banged on the door.

"I have to get my coat."

"You'll get poison."

"Throw my coat out. I don't want to come in the room. I only want my coat."

She wouldn't answer.

"Jean, if I have to break the door down to get in that room you'll wish you hadn't started anything." This wasn't being put on. It was said quietly and without a quiver or any emphasis. She opened the door and he came in and took his coat.

"I won't be back tonight," he said before he went out.

She did not answer.

He drove up to Harlem and waited for Dorothy outside her friend's house. The street was dirty and had a dusty and thick smell in the slow summer air. He kept waiting there and then Dorothy was turning the corner and walking toward him. She was wearing a simple cotton frock and she had black shoes on with fairly low heels. He kept staring at her and shaking his head slightly, as if he couldn't get over it. He pulled himself together when she came up to the car and he kept his eyes averted slightly. He'd have to do this from now on. He'd have to keep himself from looking at her too much. Maybe he would have to stop seeing her altogether.

They went out for supper and they ate a lot. They had steak dinners and then they chewed gum and smoked cigarettes while he drove to a movie. After the movie they drove some more. They both talked a lot. She would talk and it was easy to listen to her. When she was finished he would talk. It was easy to talk to her. Everything came easy.

Herb told her all about himself. He told her about Jean. He told her about the kind of people he had known all his life and the kind of people he knew now. He told her all about Paul and Wilda. She was very interested in Paul. Especially when he told her about Paul's wanting to go to China, she was extremely interested.

"It's curious, a guy like that. He never impressed me as being an adventurer, and then all of a sudden he wants to go to China. He said it was just to break the monotony, but I can't picture it."

"Maybe he sympathizes after all."

"No, I can't picture that either. And Wilda doesn't give him any trouble. Sometimes she's a real pain, but in general she's all right. Oh, he probably won't go after all, but even then it makes me wonder why he even thought about it."

Then he switched the subject and he told her what had happened today. He said, "I was sitting there thinking about the droops I work with and how rotten everything was in general and then I called her into the office and then I changed my mind and it was all so dumb. Then I felt sick the rest of the day—"

"Herb—"

He did not look at her.

"Herb, I want you to tell me something. Please tell me the truth."

"All right."

"Were you thinking about me today?"

Here it was. It had been coming slowly and gaining momentum and when it would come it would come with a great big bang and an explosion that would rip and tear and shoot things around, throw them up with a big boom. Here it was.

"Yes." He waited. She was waiting also. "Yes, all day long."

The car was going slowly at the edge of the road. He stopped it. She had turned slightly in the seat and was looking at him. He could not look back.

"I'm sorry, Herb. Herb, dear, I'm so very sorry. Look at me. Oh damn you, why don't you look at me. I want you to. There. Now tell me all about today and please don't lie, not even once."

"Dorothy, did you ever see a man cry? Not because he cut his finger or fell on his face, but because he just couldn't keep up any longer and just sort of broke down in tears. It must be pretty sloppy, don't, you think? Tears running down my face and I'd have to blow my nose—" He was trying hard, there was lead piled up at the roof of his mouth.

"But Herb—" She was shaking her head very slowly and then she was moving toward him and it was clear that she was trying to hold herself back, and then he was moving back away from her and they were both going for each other and at the same time they were moving away from each other. Something was pulling them away, and yet here they were trying to get at one another and it was like this for an era of agony. When it passed she was looking down at the floor and Herb was turning the ignition key.

"No, don't," she murmured, her voice like petals of a flower, dropping on silk. "I don't want to go yet."

For a while they were silent.

Her voice came to him gradually, from a whisper, "You try and try to be good, but you can't because deep inside you're bad. You're bad. I'm bad. You're bad. I'm so no-good that today I was thinking about you and I couldn't wait until I saw you tonight. And I wanted you, while I was working today I wanted you. And I want you now. And you want me, don't you?"

"No."

"Herb."

"No."

She put her hands on his face and turned his head toward her. He was in a straitjacket. She pushed herself up near him and kissed his lips. He didn't do a thing. He couldn't do anything. He sat there like a statue while she was kissing his lips.

And Dorothy was shaking her head slowly again and whispering, "I'm sure Tommy wouldn't mind. It's beautiful out here and in the factory it's so hot and dirty and all day long it's—but out here it's good and beautiful and you're good, you're so very good, Herb, and it's not wrong, I know it's not wrong. Tommy wouldn't mind, Herb, I'm sure he wouldn't. Herb—"

The guy told himself that for once he was really doing something that made him feel decent and brave and clean. He grinned at her, and at the same time little devils were tearing at his heart with pitchforks. He grinned.

Her eyelashes were touching his. She said, "Now you're acting."

He kept on grinning.

"I'll bite you," she said, moving slightly away, her eyes like those of a little girl about to steal jam.

"You better not."

"Yes."

"You—" But she put her lips against his cheeks and then she bit him.

"That hurt, do you know that, you terror? I'm gonna break your arm for that." He took her arm and twisted it. She leaned down and bit him again.

He let go her arm. She grabbed his head and pushed him back against the seat. Her eyes were laughing and dancing and begging for a little fun and a little love to break through the wall of misery and despair, and there was nothing here except a pure honest desire to snatch some joy out of the air and hold it for a while.

But even though he knew this, even though right now she was again kissing him and wanted him to make love to her, he held back. He started to laugh again and he threatened her and she threatened right back at him and said that he was a sissy and a baby and a dummy.

"And you're ugly, too. You got an ugly face, you got ugly eyes, and an ugly nose, you're just an ugly boy."

"I don't care. I want to be ugly. The uglier I am the better."

"You're nasty."

"Good."

"I bet you're a gangster, too. I bet you're a real dirty rotten no-good crook who steals from widows and orphans."

"You're damn tootin'. Boy, am I mean. I spend fifteen minutes every day writing down lists of people I hate. I just copy down every name from the telephone book."

"Ooohh, you're a rotten—" She frowned at him and tightened her lips, and shook her head like an angry sister.

"Now I'm gonna kidnap you, too."

"I'll scream."

She started to scream as he put the car in gear and started up. Then she grabbed the wheel and they zigzagged crazily from side to side. Finally he stopped the car and she jumped out. She ran back and he put the car in reverse and came up beside her.

"Hello, big boy," she said.

"If I get out of the car I'll big-boy you," he said. He started to laugh.

"Open the door."

He opened the door and she jumped in, hanging her knee on the gear shift lever.

"It serves you right," he said.

She punched him in the ribs, and he grabbed her and they wrestled in the car in the center of the road, with the door open. She was on top of him and was pummeling him when a car pulled up beside them and a man jumped out. He ran over to Herb's car and yelled, "In trouble, lady?"

"Help!" yelled Herb.

The man moved about wondering what to do. From his car, an old Buick sedan, a woman's creaky voice shouted, "Well, go ahead and rescue her! Don't stand there like a dope!"

The man jumped on the running board, and Dorothy pushed him in the face. He sat down hard in the road.

"Give 'er the gun, Butch," yelled Dorothy. "Here comes the West Side mob."

Herb, doubled over, unable to catch his breath, got the car going and they leaned their heads back and laughed silently until their wind gave out and they had to shriek. Dorothy looked back and saw the guy getting back into his Buick sedan. She put her hands to her face and her shoulders were going up and down like teeth in ice-cold water.

"Let's go real fast," she said after a while.

They did seventy. That wasn't fast enough for her. He got the car up to eighty. He nearly hit another car. He slowed down and she wanted him to go fast again. He said no. She said she was finished with him. It was getting late. They had cold drinks at a roadside stand and then Dorothy said that it was really getting late. He drove her home.

Parked on the little street, they didn't have much to say. She sat very still and he waited for her to get out of the car.

"Well?" he said.

"I just want to sit here for a while."

"Come on, scram."

"Herb, I said I wanted to sit here for a while."

"What am I supposed to do meanwhile?"

"Shut up."

He lit a cigarette. She took it from his mouth and began smoking it.

"When you're finished with that cigarette you're going to bed."

"Will you kiss me good night?"

"No."

"Why, Daddy?" She imitated Fannie Brice.

"Because, that's why, because, because."

"Then I'm not gonna go to sleep then." She did Baby Snooks pretty well.

She opened the door and stepped out. He walked with her up to her room. She was very tired now. She leaned on his shoulder. At the door of her room she held him about his middle and then looked at his arms, stiff at his sides.

"Oh, you, you make me sick," she said. She took his arms and put them about her waist. She was two inches shorter than he and when she came close to him they fitted each other very well.

He tried hard again but she was close against him now, her breathing was full and sweet, close against him, she was right in his arms, she wanted him to kiss her, very much did she want him to pull her up close and kiss her. He kept on saying, No, no, but then she had her lips just about touching his, drawing away, then coming back and touching his again, and he took a high dive from a flaming orange cloud into a soft pool of pure violet velvety sweetness. He pressed his lips against hers and pulled her up to him, forgetting everything.

Dorothy tightened her hold on him and when their lips came away she started to say something but he was very excited now, so she let him kiss her again, and again, and then she said, "If you really want to, Herb—"

"No."

She moved her lips against his cheek and murmured, "Really, Herb, if you need it so badly, it's all right. It's really all right. If you don't, you'll go back to the apartment and Jean will have the door locked again. You'll sleep on the sofa and in the morning you'll be sick. You'll be sick all day, and I don't want you to be sick. I don't want you to feel rotten. Tommy doesn't want you to be sick, either, Herb. I bet Tommy would like you a lot. I know he—"

"No, I'm going, and—"

"And?"

"I'm awfully sorry."

She wanted to tell him to turn around and bend over so she could kick him in the pants, but instead she pressed his hands hard and then he was going down the hall without even saying good night. She stood there, hearing him go down the steps, and something told her that she would never see him again. She threw herself on the bed and wanted to cry. But she could not do this. She worried about him. He was so miserable. She spent some time there hoping that things would change and he would be happy.

Then she spent time worrying about Tommy. She fell asleep worrying about all the people who were unhappy.

CHAPTER V

George Green was doing all right for himself. He waited for Jean to come out of the bedroom, and while he waited he mixed himself a few drinks and then he looked at his wristwatch, which told him that it was getting nice and late. If anyone thought a job like this Jean was bad, they were crazy. He began comparing her with other women he had slept with, and he told himself that she was one of the best. Give her time and she would really amount to something, this girl. He wondered what her husband looked like. That was one of the things she didn't want to talk about. All he knew of the husband was that he was an assortment of dirty names and also a rat, a skunk, and a pretty low article in general.

But he must have money. This was a classy layout, this apartment. That orange piano was something. The rug was something. The liquor was no junk. And Jean didn't buy those dresses and shoes and hats with leaves from the trees.

Things weren't bad then, figured George. He wasn't working, but he had this loan of three hundred from brother-in-law Dan, the sucker, and he had a little, very little, coming from the old man. He knew at least ten saps from school, or clubs, or places and parties he had been to, who would advance him a few bucks, if for nothing more than to get him out of their hair. He took another drink and then purred, "Oh, am I lonesome—"

"Just another minute—" she called from the bedroom.

"Just another minute and I'll die from the blues."

She made a face. If this guy would keep his mouth shut more he wouldn't be so bad. But he really lacked brains. It was a wonder what the colleges were putting out nowadays. She sighed and went into the parlor.

About ten minutes later the door opened and Herb walked in. Jean pushed George away and jumped to her feet. George got up and clenched his fists.

"You said you were staying away tonight," said Jean.

"I changed my mind." He ignored George. "I'm going to sleep, if you don't mind. Don't make too much noise."

"What's the big idea?" said George. He had to say something. He wanted to pick up this little guy and throw him out of the room into the hall. He wanted to show Jean he could do something like that.

Herb waited a moment and then he said, "Do you have any complaints to make? We have an office downstairs. Call them if you don't like the service, or if anyone is annoying you."

"Who is this guy?" said George, turning to Jean. He made himself sound tough.

"Oh, don't be dumb," Jean said.

"He's sort of young, isn't he, Jean?" Herb's eyebrows went up.

"What are you, funny?" said George. He took a step forward, but Jean grabbed his wrist.

"Please don't start any trouble, Herb." Jean's voice was imploring. She knew Herb. She knew what he could do. Once he had gotten in a fight with a truckdriver and she had never seen anything like it. The truckdriver must have weighed about two hundred and it was muscle and hard bone. When the fight was over the truckdriver had picked himself off the road and had shaken Herb's hand and said, "Buddy, you can really fight." And that wasn't the only time. But she remembered it because the truckdriver had been so big and had looked so tough, and had started the fight after hitting Herb's fender trying to cut him out.

She was still holding George Green's wrist. "Won't you please go now, Herb?"

"Okay. I'll go in the bedroom and leave you two alone. But don't make too much noise."

He began to go into the bedroom, but George pulled himself away from Jean and said, "You're too funny." He grabbed Herb by the shoulders and swung him around. "She don't want you around, see? She told me all about you, smart guy. She's too good for a little snake like you. Get out while the getting's good."

Herb looked at Jean. "Has he been drinking? I want to take all these things into consideration, you know."

George moved forward and pushed Herb in the face. It was a hard push and Herb sat down. He got up very slowly. George pushed him in the face again.

"Don't, George! Don't start!" Jean was watching Herb very closely. He was getting up again.

George moved in once more and this time Herb, from a low crouch, went for his knees. He yanked up and then put his shoulder against George's legs. The big guy went down and while he was still falling Herb moved up on him and chopped an elbow into his ribs. George squirmed away and Herb waited. Then when George turned, Herb smashed him under the ear, then under the heart, then in the jaw again and George went down. Herb ran at him, jumped, and landed with his heels on the blonde boy's nose and teeth.

"Unfair—coward—" George was spitting blood.

"Balls."

The big boy was all excited now. And he was hurt. He managed to get away from under Herb and then he came up fast and they tussled about and fell over a few chairs and Jean saw George pick Herb up over his shoulder in a flying mare hold and throw him up and down. Herb landed hard but squirmed away from the next one and then got in a few hard punches that hurt. George backed away as Herb came in close. Then he let go a left jab that was much too slow and Herb came in under it and slammed him in the ribs, right-hooked him to the jaw, right-hooked him again, straightened his wavering body with a short left, then brought the right home again, to the point of the jaw, knocking him out.

Green fell with a big thump, flat on his back. He was stretched out cold on the floor. Herb looked over at Jean. She had one hand across her mouth like one of the blonde heroines in a movie thriller.

"That wasn't so bad, was it?" said Herb. He looked at his knuckles. They hurt, but they weren't cracked. They hurt comfortably.

"He's really hurt," said Jean.

"Yeah, I guess he is. Better put some cold water on him. I'm going to sleep. I'm a little tired."

"Wait—help me with him."

"Look. Just throw a little water on him and send him home to mother. Give him a kiss for me before he goes."

"But he's really—"

Herb closed the bedroom door. He got undressed and then when he went to the bathroom he saw that Jean was holding George erect over the washbasin and blood was coming from his nose.

Herb pulled George back and said, "Get him a handkerchief. Get about five of them."

"My nose is bleeding," said George. He was in pain. His eyes were shut tightly, and a lot of blood was coming from his nose.

"Hurts, doesn't it?" said Herb, holding a handkerchief beneath the cold-water faucet and then putting it up to George's nose.

"Yeah, it hurts, and don't think I'm finished with you. I never forget anything like this."

His face looked messed up. His eyes were all right, but his lips were swollen and blood was all over his chin. And his nose had seen better days.

"Keep holding a handkerchief to it on your way home. Keep your head back," said Herb.

"You're gonna see more of me." George pressed the handkerchief against his nose and tilted his head back. He walked that way through to the hall door and Jean came up to him. She said, "Call me up tomorrow and tell me how you feel."

"All right, darling. Kiss me."

Herb watched them. He wanted to laugh, but he figured he'd give them a break and let them finish the scene without interruption. He went back to the bathroom and took a quick shower and drank a glass of cold water, then washed his teeth with a powder that produced a mint tang and clean taste in his mouth, and after that a mouthwash and gargle. He liked doing this, little things like brushing his teeth and gargling with mouthwash, or running that rubber scalp brush over his head, or shaving with that fine Swiss razor that Paul had given him for Christmas.

He drank another glass of water, and went into the bedroom. He heard the outer door close and in a few minutes Jean came into the room. She stood in the doorway looking at him as he rested easily with his hands behind his head.

"Put the light out," he said.

She put the light out and walked over to the other bed. He turned over and yawned.

"Good night," he said. He didn't listen to see if she would answer. But he did hear her pushing back the sheets and smoothing the pillow, patting it to make a place for her head.

"Good night," she said.

Soon she was sitting up and looking at him as he slept. She couldn't sleep herself, it was so hot, and her mind was buzzing. She sat there looking at him.

CHAPTER VI

They were being hammered back, split in two, smashed against the sea to come struggling back, moving down, moving up, trying to gain a foothold and dig in to put up a fight. There were the fliers being blown out of the sky but coming back and trying to do something. There were the veterans, very few of them by now, still holding the vantage trenches and fighting in the heat and summer dust with their scarred hands and punctured bodies. And there were the youngsters, the kids coming from training camps, marching into the well of trench mortar and explosive bullets. Behind all of them were the people, running, shrieking, crouching and trying to get away from the bombs, the shells. And above them, before them, coming on, each day getting something done, the enemy moved forward. At times they moved forward many miles. At times they moved across yards of mud and steel and blood. But they were always moving. They were always gaining ground. The trenches were moved back. The artillery was shoved around like chessmen. The maps were studied carefully to see if there wasn't a chance here, a chance there. The ammunition was brought in, faster, faster, the calls for help, the calls for bandages, the plea for guns and more tanks, more men, they came from the lead-colored lips of the men in the trenches and the generals in the trenches with the men.

There was a lot of trouble and a lot of wonder. There were the splits in the towns and the splits in the hearts of many soldiers. They were tired and they were afraid. They wanted to stop it already. But there is always this. After a while men get tired, even when they know what they are fighting for and when they believe in it. They get tired and they want to lie down and take a rest.

And yet the great number still wanted to fight. They wanted to fight even more now than when they had first come up to the front. They wanted to kill and as individual units they had lost their identity, both to themselves and to their comrades. They were welded into this thin struggling line on the front, their bayonets pointed as one great weapon, their eyes aimed as one great searching light.

The men of the International Brigade were still in it. Now they were digging in, marching around, stopping and firing, moving forward and then retreating, in a practical, cold and expressionless project, trying to stop this force coming at them in newly developed motorized units, new planes, machine guns, new cannons smashing at them in artillery bombardment which knew no end, which smoked up the sky of Spain and threw white puffs into the air.

These men of the International Brigade had been fighting for a long time. Americans, Canadians, Irish, English, French, Cubans, men from all over the world, exiles from Germany and Italy, college students, professors, scholars, poets, engineers, chemists, skilled laborers, unskilled laborers, they had been fighting for a long time. They had accomplished some fine things at Madrid and Brunete and in the skirmishes to the north. Now they were leavened, many had gone down just a few yards from an Insurgent trench, many were blown up by bombs, and in groups smashed by a shell. The foreign volunteers had been hard hit in this Spring offensive.

But they were still in it. And on a hill a few hundred yards away from the Insurgents two thousand of them were getting ready for a defensive maneuver that would split the oncoming wave and perhaps make way for a new trench line.

The attack was expected in a few hours. The men relaxed. They would need all available strength in the hand-to-hand fighting that would probably ensue. There was little talk. The few officers kept making their rounds, and occasionally spoke simple words of encouragement. But that was old stuff. It was not needed. These men did not need pep talks. They knew what they were fighting for, and they knew exactly what they had to do. They were engaged in a very important business over here and there was no time to waste in superfluous adjustment to the situation. It was old stuff. They were getting ready now.

One of them made himself comfortable in a soft part of the trench. He took out a pad and pencil and began writing. At first he wrote slowly, as if he did not have anything else to do and was just trying to get rid of time. But then he set his eyes hard on the paper. His fingers gripped the pencil hard.

"… then I tell myself that I must not feel this way, that you do not want me to feel any other way than how I felt when I first told you I was going. But even then it is really hard not to get weak when I think of you back there. I want to hit my head up against the wall and tell myself that you will be very angry for me telling you what a coward I am at times. But I am really not a coward. That's a crazy way of putting it, because you really do not have a line separating bravery and cowardice. The only coward here is the man who falls intentionally, or who sneaks away during the night. And even then there were nights when I wanted to sneak away, or there were days when I wanted to wound myself and get myself put on a boat and sent back to you. They did not last long, these times when I felt that way. But I still felt that way, and even though I do not feel that way now (if you could see where I am now, honey, you would know damn well why I can't afford to feel that way) I know that later I will want to do something to make them send me back to you. I want to see you so badly, I want you really so much I want to see you again dear Dorothy darling please why can't they stop why can't we beat them now why is it that I want to—to …"

He scribbled over the paper and tore it from the pad. He jumbled it up in his hands, tore it in little pieces and threw it at the muddy wall of the trench.

He kept looking at the little pieces of paper falling down slowly across the stones and mud of the trench wall.

There was a hiss, then a shout, a screech, another hiss. A runner was being sent back over the hill. A few shells began to drop near and along the line on the hill. The massed infantry behind the hill began their flanking movement. Up in front the troops began to climb over the parapet as the Insurgents started to fire. A Loyalist plane appeared from a cloud and another one was beside it, dipping, then swooping upwards, down, raking the first enemy trench.

The cross fire was disconcerted at first, but then the rebel gunners found themselves, and they sighted the first wave and began putting them down. The figures running forward in that irregular line began dropping as the mouths of the machine guns kept on gulping at the belts of bullets.

More shells and trench mortars popped down or screeched across the area dividing the two forces. From behind and to the left there started another movement, and the rebels saw tanks crawling. There was a shout at first, but the order from behind the lines came fast, telling them to hold the first line of trenches at all costs.

The Loyalists moved forward. They were falling fast but they were still moving forward. It had started out as a defensive maneuver, but the rebels were committing suicide by holding that first trench line. The order came to wipe them out and keep on going.

Some of the rebels started something by climbing out of the trench and running away. More followed. A few of the machine guns were silenced in this way. The Loyalists, dropping and running, men dropping and men running, falling, getting up and running some more, came up to the first trench, jabbed their bayonets, leaped across and kept on going.

The tanks moved over to one side, men were running almost in a straight line, and far behind them the trucks were being loaded with men to get them up faster, the shouts and screams, the bullets and shells and noise of airplanes covering this flat land was mixed in with the dust from heavy boots, and blood from fallen men.

The Government forces kept on going.

They knew what had to be done now. The second line had to be taken. The reinforcements were to outflank the rebels to the left and shove them back, and then the tanks would rip them apart and the planes would get them before they could organize a retreat. If they tried to come up again their own machine guns, now in hands of the Loyalists, would be aimed at them.

In that second line of trenches the Insurgents made their stand. They worked fast and began firing. The Loyalists came on. They started to fall. But they still came on. The rebels in that second line were working very fast now. They were using up a lot of bullets but then as the seconds clicked by and the line came nearer and nearer they knew somehow that they were not going to stop men coming over to kill them.

From three thousand feet an airplane dived, kept on going down toward a line in the brown ground, then swooped by, seeming to graze the helmets of the men in the trench line. The machine gun raked up and down, the men fell, another plane came along, the men screamed and tried to dig themselves underneath the trench, into a place where no bullets came.

But this was a well-planned attack from the air. Again the planes came. They seemed to be going around in a circle and every time they moved down near the rebel lines the guns barked out and the bullets went down and killed the men. They began jumping out of the trench and running away. They ran toward the third trench line and then the Loyalist wave reached the second trench, and when the rebels began to come back they were caught. The Loyalists mowed them down, then moved toward that third trench. They were started now. Like a great reaping machine they came forward, men, tanks, planes, and the rebels were forced back. The trucks kept coming up to the front with more Government soldiers, the rebels began an almost riotous retreat, and then, as the flanking maneuver took on monstrous potentialities, and the Insurgents were forced into a trap long planned by Government strategists, there came a final tremendous drive, which lasted until early evening. The prisoners were sent back, new lines were put up, more men were being sent up to the advanced front, and from the dust-filled, gasping throats of the first line of men there came a cry, a sigh, a choked sob.

"Well, Tommy?"

"This means something."

"Where's Pete?"

"He went down. I saw him. He was one of the first."

"Say, look at your arm, Tommy."

"Oh. I didn't see that."

"It's bleeding bad. And look, your side—"

"Yeah. Look at it. Look at that blood coming. Look at that damned blood."

"Hey! First aid! First aid!"

"It's all—right. I—can bandage—"

"First aid! Over here!"

They came up and put Tommy on a stretcher. He was bleeding a lot.

CHAPTER VII

For two weeks Herb made himself stay away from Dorothy. He tried hard, and managed to work himself into a schedule of labor and interesting activities which took his mind off her. At the office he put in eight hard hours a day, and in the evenings he went to the movies, he hung around bars, he talked a lot, he hunted up casual friends and spent time with them, he did a lot of reading and most of his time was absorbed in this way.

He was staying now in a Midtown hotel. He had written a brief note to Jean on the morning following the trouble with George Green, and he merely wrote her that he was staying at this hotel, and he gave the address in case she wanted to get in touch with him.

His room in the hotel was well-aired and he could look out on Seventh Avenue and see the people walking fast, and the cars jolting, darting forward and grazing each other. From this room he could look down ten stories and see the excitement and the hurry and all the trouble that was going on down there.

In the evening he would read for a while in the room and it was quiet as he sat down by the window and read the *Telegraph*. He would look over the front page and read about all the trouble and death and the problems, the vast puzzles which made faces at him from the headlines. The whole thing amounted to a mess. He had concluded this many years before, and at times since he had started going with Jean, even before that, when he had first gotten this job, he had definitely come to that conclusion. But he never dwelt upon it. He agreed with himself that this way, it was just a big mess, and then he forgot about it and joined in the misery. When all was said and done, he was just one of the boys, and what happened to them had to happen to him. Sooner or later everybody was in for a terrific jerking around. You couldn't run away from it. It always caught up with you.

Here were people getting killed in transcontinental air liners. Here was one that had smashed into a Rocky Mountain peak and had taken eleven people down with it to death. Some of those men and women must have felt pretty good before that plane went down. They must have been going to see relatives, or just going on a vacation, or maybe going out to the Coast to sign a big contract. Maybe some of them felt low. They might have been in trouble. Then the plane went down and the whole rigamajig was over and done with. It didn't make a bit of difference how they had felt. It was all over now.

He put the paper down and took a look back on himself. He thought of his years at Columbia. That had been all right. It was a pleasant interval, when troubles came one on top of the other, but they were small and you could laugh while you were having them. Flunking a quiz, lending out a tux and not getting it back, getting called down to the Dean's office for being overcut, getting snubbed by a not-too-pretty girl over the phone, betting ten bucks on a football game and seeing a dumb quarterback throw it away in four dumb plays.

Coming back to him now were those workless days when he did not know what was coming next, when he started to play baseball and had knocked around in Maryland with this semi-pro team and then had come up to New York again and had played a fairly clean game at short for a fairly good team. It was a laughing matter now, as he looked back on it. He was playing twilight games, and sometimes he made fifteen bucks a game. Some weeks he made fifty bucks, and it was a cinch. The team manager was a smart boy, and he knew how to make people pay money to see the games.

But then that last year at Columbia, and the postgraduate course in journalism, and finally the beginning of real trouble and real wonder, then going through years of jumping around trying to get adjusted, and finally this, sitting here and wondering what was going to happen next.

His phone rang. It was Paul. He was downstairs in the lobby. He came up and boomed into the room.

"What you doin' here?"

"Didn't she tell you?"

"I haven't seen her," said Paul. He emphasized "seen." "Wilda was talking to her and she said you had gone here."

"Is that all she said?"

"That's all Wilda told me." Paul looked around the room. He was curious and very interested. He sat down and put a handkerchief to his forehead. He looked questioningly at Herb.

"She brought a guy into the apartment," said Herb. He had his eyes on the floor. "It was okay with me, but the guy was young and he wanted to be brave. So he started trouble and we had a little aggravation there. It was more or less of a payoff. I don't know. I didn't want to go, but I didn't even want to see the place anymore. I wanted to get away from it. I don't mind this."

"Why don't you get in touch with a guy?" said Paul. Herb brought a bottle out from his bureau drawer and then he rang for the bellboy. Paul took a drink straight and said, "You had a fight with him?"

Herb nodded. He took a drink. Right now he felt like talking a lot. There was really very much that he wanted to say but it was a question whether or not Paul was the person to say it to. Paul was probably all right. He could use a little more brains at times, and he could show a little more life and be more entertaining at times, but he was probably all right. Herb took another drink. The bellboy came in and was sent out for some charged water and ice. Paul took another drink.

"Don't tell me you're going to stay here," said Paul.

"Maybe I will. It's not so bad. I don't mind it too much."

"It's really a shame about you and Jean," said Paul clumsily.

Herb did not answer. He went over to the window with another drink in his hand and he looked out over the street and buildings and saw the evening glow up there, pink and light blue, with a flare of green in one of the big signs. Soon it would be dark and all the lights would go on, beckoning him and others to come out and join in the fun before another droopy day started.

The bellboy came in and Herb tipped him a half-dollar.

"What's Jean going to do?" Paul was saying.

"I don't care what she does."

Paul squirted soda into the glass of ice and Scotch.

"Jesus Christ," he said. He took a long drink and shook his head slowly. Herb's eyebrows went up slightly and he wondered why Paul felt so low all of a sudden.

"How're things with you?" he said.

"Bad." Paul's mouth was near the glass. "Can't keep my mind on my work."

"No?"

"Herb, I have a tough job, you know? I have a real tough job." He finished the glass and nodded. "A real tough job. My work is really work, don't kid yourself about that. When I get finished, the day's over, I feel tired, real tired."

"Well, that's good. That's the way it should be. Then you—"

"Then I come home and Wilda's got a good meal cooked. That is, two days out of the week she cooks dinner for us, and I take it easy and read for a while. Then she wants to go out. She's got three million friends and to hear her talk they can't go on living without her. When we're not visiting we're going to the movies. We're going to crazy restaurants where the music is either Russian or Turkish or Indian, I don't know. We get back real late and the next morning I get up and there's another day in front of me."

Paul filled his glass again. He took more Scotch this time. He rambled on and talked a lot. Herb listened to him and it went in one ear and out the other. It could have been interesting at another time, perhaps. But not right now, because Herb did not particularly care whether or not Paul and Wilda would ever have any children just as soon Wilda decided that they had enough money to send the kid to one of the better New England schools and then to Dartmouth and then to Europe to study, and now Paul was thirty-seven and Wilda was thirty and by the time they had enough money to go and give the kid a first-class send-off they might not be able to have the kid in the first place. Paul laughed and said he got a kick out of it but it didn't particularly worry him because one of these days Wilda would forget to do something or other and first thing she knew she'd wake up one morning feeling funny and before she knew it she'd have to begin looking around for a carriage and a maid. And even if they never got a kid, Paul went on, it was nothing to cry about. So you went and had a kid and then you had another one and a third and the three of them played you for a sucker for twenty-two or three years, and then wrote you or came to see you whenever they needed dough. Paul said that it was probably a rotten thing to claim, but it was really that way, so perhaps it was all for the best that he and Wilda were having no children. And yet again—

Paul was talking more to himself than to Herb. They were both drinking evenly and paying much attention to the liquor in the bottle and the liquor in their mouths. They were finishing this first fifth.

"Open up the window," said Paul. "It's hot in here."

"The window's open wide now. I can't open it any wider."

"It's hot, you know? Let's go out."

"Where's Wilda?"

"Oh—"

"Where is she?"

"Well, look," said Paul, "Wilda told me, you see—she said maybe it would be—well, she told me to come over here and see you. See, it's—"

"Oh, then she's with Jean."

"I guess she is, I guess—"

"But she won't be with Jean very long. She'll want you coming back soon, won't she?" He got a good look at Paul, but Paul was carrying it all right. They were well into the second bottle now.

"Aw, it's all right," Paul was saying, "it's all right."

"Okay, let's go out."

They went out and walked over to a bar where there was a fairly intelligent crowd of men. It was a very simple layout here, and they served good sea food and once while a waiter would come over and say that they had some fine lamb chops today, but that he would not advise the squab. The lamb chops were really very nice, however. It was a quiet place and very seldom did anyone laugh unless there was something really funny to laugh about.

Herb and Paul came in and stood at the polished oak bar. The place was comfortably cool and although it was past eight there were quite a few men eating at the thick oak tables that bordered the room.

"Hello, Mr. Hervey—Mr. Schuen."

"Hello, Bill. H'mm, sort of late, isn't it?"

The bartender looked closely at Herb. He wanted to ask him if he had eaten yet, because he knew right well that Herb had not eaten, and that he had been drinking a lot already. And it seemed to be the same way with Paul. They were both steady and they probably felt all right now, but they should have eaten something.

"Well, it's past supper time, Mr. Hervey."

"Yeah, it is, isn't it? Funny, I didn't have supper. I forgot to eat. I just—"

Paul asked for drinks. The bartender waited for Herb to say that he would eat something first, but Herb was silent and the Scotch was brought up across the bar. There were other men at the bar, so Bill could not stay there and make suggestions.

Now the place was a little more noisy but not from raised voices. There were more men coming into the place and the tables were being cleared. They were at the bar. They ranged along the thick oak and the brass rail and drank and talked.

In the three years he had known Paul, Herb had enjoyed some interesting evenings with him. But it was not Paul himself who had made the evenings interesting. It was the people they had met and the things that had happened to them. There were parties and gatherings, there were a few stag parties that Paul had taken him to, there were five or six evenings something like this when they had been out together.

But those other times had been cut off suddenly, with Paul going home to Wilda, and Herb going home to Jean. When the two couples were out together, there was very little excitement and not much enjoyment. Usually there was trouble. Herb put down his glass now and reflected on that party several weeks ago, when he had found it necessary to throw a punch at Jean, and when she had thrown that ginger ale highball in his face, tried to kick him in the stomach. Reflecting upon it, he began to talk about it.

"That's how it really started. It started before that, it really started the first day I saw her. But it started that night. And it ended that night. You see what I mean? It started and it ended that same night."

"Yeah, I see what you mean. You know, Jean has a temper that you got to be careful of. Now it just occurs to me now, you know, just thinking about it, I remember that I was sitting there and watching her and any minute I knew she was going to blow up. You see, you were saying something about how nice she was, or how nice her hair was, or her teeth. I don't know, something like that. And you made a slip. I don't remember, but it didn't sound so good. Then this guy Vincents made a remark and you answered him back and Jean said something and you said something and I said to myself here it comes and there it was. She was throwing that glass of liquor square in your face."

"It was a ginger ale highball."

"Yeah, that's what it was all right. It was a ginger ale highball."

"Then I hit her, didn't I?"

"Yeah, you hit her, all right. You cracked her across the mouth with the back of your hand."

Herb leaned low over the bar and looked at the heavy grain in the dull polished oak. "Maybe I shouldn't have done that."

"Then," Paul said, "the trouble started. You were sort of dopey yourself after that. I guess it hurt you as much as it hurt her. But you're lucky she didn't reach you when she kicked. If that shoe of hers would've caught you in the stomach it might have done a lot of harm."

"It might have done a lot of good."

Paul moved his arm for another drink and Herb looked at the bartender and nodded. They stood there quietly putting them down one after another and then the bartender was talking to them but they were not listening. They were talking to each other about things that had happened long ago and Paul was doing most of the talking. Then, somehow, they were in another bar. They were out of there also and in another bar. They were in two more bars. They were in a place, sitting down at a table and still drinking. They were in that place for an hour, and then they were moving west in the Forties and they were in another place. It was late now, about eleven-thirty, and this place was fairly well filled, but Herb and Paul saw nothing but the bottle and the glasses and each other's face, across the table. They heard nothing, even though there was a lot of noise in this place, and a few women and girls not long out of high school were putting up a good show with three or four thick cocktails in them, and the four-star phonies with greasy wavy hair and too-long, much too-draped double-breasted suits with pegged trousers and very little money in those trousers, were talking loud and talking big and telling old jokes and making cracks with plenty of filth and very little humor.

But Herb and Paul, oblivious to all this, sat at a table in a neglected corner and talked while they leaned over the glasses. Paul put up his hand to stop Herb, who was talking about a horse that he knew had been doped.

"Now I wanna say something, and I'm gonna say it because I wanna say it and I should say it. You understand that?"

"Absolutely. If there's something you want to say you have the right to say it. You got every right in the world. We're not living in Germany or Italy or Russia or Japan or France or China or—"

"So I wanna say this. Now, you lissen while I talk because it's really something that I want you to hear. It's really something that you should know and I should tell you. It's about Jean. Now you know when I knew Jean? I knew that girl when she was a baby. You never knew that, did you? Because I didn't want you to know it. And Jean didn't want you to know it. But now you know it. Sure, we were playmates, or not that, we were friends. She was a little baby and I was nine years old. Now you wouldn't believe that, would you? You wouldn't believe it, would you? But that's the truth. And you know where it was? It was right here in New York State. It was in Albany. They lived there and we lived—well we knew each other, because our families—well, I saw her a lot and then when I was at Massachusetts Tech she was there for a dance and we began to talk and we found out who each other was. Now would you believe that? So then we kept in touch with each other and then I graduated and joined the air service and I was sent up to Mitchel Field and so I saw her again. I saw her a lot of times. I took her out a few times and then guess what she told me. Guess what Jean told me. She really told me that she was in love with me and that we should go ahead and get married. So I figured that I figured that maybe it would be all right to wait awhile before I got well before I—"

"Well?"

"But I didn't want to marry Jean."

"Well?"

"I said I just said that I—"

"Come on, tell me what happened after that. You were at Mitchel Field and she wanted to marry you."

"But then I got out of the Army and I started to fly commercial. See, I—"

"Come on, what about Jean?"

"Oh, well, I loved Jean, see? And I still love her. I love Jean, I—you know something, I really love that girl, and now if you—"

"Oh, now I see. You're telling me that you love Jean."

"That's it."

"I see." He poured himself a drink and poured more over his hand than went into the glass.

Paul reached for the bottle. "So I wanted to go to China, anywhere, not only China I want to go anywhere because I love Jean and I don't want to to—I want to—you see, there's Wilda, and there's you, and I didn't want to say—" He fell back in the chair and his eyes were wide and badly shot now. He tried to shake his head, but it was no use trying to do anything, because whatever he tried to do, he would only end by falling to the floor, out cold. He did this. He tried to stand up. He went over like a log and fell on the floor. His arms moved out and he was still. Herb sat there staring at him while the waiters came over to pick him up.

They picked him up and began carrying him to the door. Herb started after them. He caught one of them by the collar and said, "He's all right. He's my friend. I'm telling you he's all right."

"Put them in a cab, Joe," said one of the waiters. "There's a cab."

"Find out where they live."

"Say, what's the idea? We don't want to go home," said Herb.

The waiters walked back into the place. In the cab Herb lurched toward the front seat and shouted, "Drive up to Harlem. Go on, I—"

"Where?"

"Just keep on driving."

It took a long time, but finally Herb found the street. He told the driver to wait, and he tried to pull Paul out of the cab. But Paul was too heavy and he was sleeping. Herb stumbled into the tenement and up the steps and knocked on her door.

She came to the door without asking who was there and when she saw Herb she put her arms out to catch him from falling. She nearly fell back herself with his sodden weight now, and she dragged him over to the bed and there let him rest.

"You had to do this before you could come up and see me," she said.

He pushed himself up and swayed beside the bed, looking down on her.

"I got a friend outside. Can't leave my friend."

"You can ask him in."

"Okay. I'll go down and tell him to come in."

She held him back. If she let him go he might fall down all the stairs. She put on a torn tweed coat and ran outside. She said to the cab driver, "Did they pay?"

The cab driver looked back at her and figured that even if they were soaked these guys were doing all right. He shook his head and Dorothy opened the back door. She took money out of Paul's pocket and paid the driver.

"It's all right. You don't have to wait," she said.

Paul was out of the cab now, kneeling on the pavement.

"Come on, we'll take a walk," said Dorothy. She helped him up. They went in and up the steps. Then they were in her room and Paul was stretched out on the bed. Herb was standing up and trying to get himself out of it.

It was this way. Dorothy was putting the torn tweed coat back in the closet and Paul was out again. Herb stood there looking at Dorothy in her white nightgown, her long black hair gleaming around her shoulders, her face, that face.

"Lie down and go to sleep," Dorothy was saying.

"I'm not tired," Herb said.

She stepped quickly over to him and pushed him down on the bed. "Now," she said, and slapped him with all her might across the face, "that makes me feel better."

Herb's eyes were closed and he had not even felt it. He was going to sleep now, and Dorothy pushed him over against Paul and then got down next to him. She put her arms around his neck and kissed his cheek. She looked at his closed eyes, his nose, his lips. She kissed him again.

In the morning Paul was pretty sick. He got up at seven and woke Dorothy up. He did not know where he was and he was not trying hard to find out. She showed him the bathroom but even when he came out he was still sick. Herb was awakened by the noise and he knew what had happened and understood why he felt now as if he was pumped full of flour and water, and the watered flour was trying to force its way out of his head. He saw that Dorothy was dressed already.

Paul was sitting down on the bed, holding his head. Dorothy said, "I have to go to work now."

"Call a cab for us," said Herb.

She called the cab and waited until it came. Herb and Paul got in and then Dorothy left them and walked over to the subway.

At the apartment house where the Schuens lived the cab stopped. Paul said that he was perfectly all right now and that Herb should go on and leave him alone. But Herb went up to the apartment with Paul, and Wilda was there waiting for them. There were rings under her eyes and she had slept only a few hours. Her voice was tired and yet it was loud.

"Couldn't you have called me up?"

"I had a little too much," said Paul. "I'm still loaded, I guess. Can't go in to work."

"Where were you?"

"We sort of forgot ourselves," said Paul.

"Where did you stay all night?"

"We were over my place," said Herb.

She looked from Paul to Herb to Paul and back to Herb. Her eyes stabbed at Herb. "You're a liar. I called up your place and Jean told me all about you."

"I mean he was over my room at the hotel."

"Oh, he was over your room at the hotel."

"That's all," said Paul. "We started to drink and we forgot ourselves."

"Listen, you—" Wilda was very much upset. She kept looking at Paul and talking to Herb. "You're no good. I asked Paul to go over there and have a talk with you. I'm Jean's best friend and I was trying to fix things up. But you're no good, and you go out of your way to look for trouble. Don't worry, either. Jean told me what was what. And I can see the proof of it when I send my husband, your friend, over to have a sensible talk with you and you go and get him so drunk his eyes are full of blood and he don't look good, he's sick—" Her voice was full, her lips jelled convulsively.

Paul said, "I'm not sick."

"You are, you are." Wilda, her face lined, teeth biting lips trying to keep self-control, clutched at him and hugged him. "Oh Paul, Paul—"

She started to sob.

"What's all the excitement about?" Herb moved toward the door.

Wilda held Paul to one side. She shouted, "That's right, get out. Get out of here."

"I'm getting," said Herb. He shrugged slightly as he went out. He took a cab over to the hotel and took a bath, put on a different suit and then went down to the grill and had two large glasses of tomato juice. He felt fairly steady and was not too tired as he entered the office.

In the Schuens' apartment Wilda made Paul undress. Half her questions he would not answer. Once he asked her to leave him alone until he felt better, and they would talk the whole thing over. But she kept on nagging him and telling him how disappointed she was in him, and how rotten Herb was. At last he said, "Lay off for a while, will you? Yelling at me doesn't do no good." Yet she kept on, and even while he was in the cold shower, he could hear her outside the glass-enclosed shower chamber, yelling at him through the glass.

But while she was doing all this talking, she was getting him out of it, making him drink a sizzling glass of alkaline powders in cold water, and then putting ice to his head.

Finally he said that he was all right. He would go to the office. Wilda stood at the window and watched him walk across the street, four stories below. Oh, Paul, you're so good, you're so good, I love to worry about you.

On the street, taking his time, Paul kept wondering what he had said last night that was bothering him so much now. He had said something that was coming back to him now and daring him to guess what it was. Over his desk splattered with paper and ink and steel instruments, he went back over last night and tried hard to remember but it evaded him, jumping away and mocking the short reach of his mind. Toward noontime he felt sick again, and from then on until he came home at night he did not feel good. He had little to say to Wilda, and was relieved when she said that she did not care if they went to bed early tonight.

Waiting there, still waiting at nine o'clock, Dorothy knew that Herb would come. He might not come until eleven, but he would see her tonight and tell her what was wrong, why he had come up last night, drunk with his drunken friend.

Her friends down the street had wanted her to go with them to a meeting tonight. It was an important anti-Nazi rally, and there would be some good speakers and moving pictures of war action in Spain and China, and also photographs of military strength in Czechoslovakia, Russia, France and England. There would also be ten members of the Abraham Lincoln Battalion just returned wounded from Spain. It was something she had wanted to see very much. But instead she was up here now in her room waiting for Herb to come.

At half-past nine he came.

"I was expecting you," she said.

"I know. That's why I came."

"How do you feel?"

"I'm all right now. Is there anything at all I can do to make up for the way I acted last night?"

"Who was the other bum?"

"That was Paul."

"Oh, so that was Paul," she said, "that was the one who wanted to go to China."

"Yes."

"Why didn't you bring him here when I could talk to him?"

"I will. I'd like you to talk to him. You see, I found out a lot about him last night that I never knew before. He's really quite a guy. He's one of the most decent men I've ever known. And I didn't realize that until last night, when he said a few things that he will never remember. He told me that he was in love with Jean, and he said that when he was practically out on his feet. I sort of felt that something was wrong, but I could never put my finger on it. I could see that things were sort of strained when Jean and Paul were in the same room, but I never really thought much about it. Now it's as clear as daylight. She's been putting the pressure on and the harder he tries to keep away from her the more she goes after him."

"She seems to be giving everybody a lot of trouble."

"I don't know what I should do about Paul. But I can't see myself telling him that he let it all out to me."

"Herb, why haven't you been up to see me? Do you know, I was so sore at you last night that I slapped you. Maybe you felt it this morning."

He shook his head. "Why were you angry?"

"Because you haven't been up to see me. And when you do come up—"

There are some things which must be said, which you know must come out and be heard. But they remain deep no matter how hard you work digging for them. They won't come out. Sometimes they are expressed in your eyes, sometimes they are not even expressed although they are realized mutually. And yet there are times when they won't budge. They remain buried.

He nodded. "You're right. I should have come up to see you."

"Then why didn't you?"

He wondered how it would sound if he said it.

"Herb, why didn't you?"

"Because I don't like you."

"I don't like you either."

"You—"

"Herb, I'm not kidding now. I want to know why you didn't come up to see me for two weeks. I was awfully lonesome for you. Tommy hasn't written and I've been all alone and I was even sick. You're just a mean thing."

"I just didn't feel like seeing you. I—" He couldn't keep it up any longer, because he had to look at her, and he had to stand there near her, talking like this.

"Well, then, I don't feel like seeing you either."

"No?"

"No."

"I'll go then."

"Go," she said, "and I hope you fall down all the steps and break your neck."

He started to go. Then he whirled around and rushed up to her. He grabbed Dorothy and said, "Take that back."

He grabbed her more tightly.

"You're hurting me, you bully."

He picked her up and threw her on the bed. He jumped on top of her and they started to wrestle. She sprawled on top of him and held his head straight and then lowered her lips to kiss him.

"No, Dorothy, please. Please, I don't want to. I—"

"Yes."

"Please, no."

"Then you don't like me to kiss you. You don't like the way I kiss. According to you I don't even know how to kiss."

"That's it. You don't know how to kiss. Get up off me."

She got up and in doing so she purposely kneed him in the stomach. He groaned as she pulled him to his feet and then he said, "What should we do tonight?"

"I was supposed to go to a big meeting but on account of you I didn't go, you dog."

"Well, it's still early. You can still make it."

"You got your car?"

"Sure."

"Do you want to go?"

They were walking down the stairs, hand in hand. "What kind of meeting is it?" he said.

"Oh, it's sort of radical. You'd call it a gang of bearded bomb-throwers getting ready to blow up the White House. I don't think you'd be interested."

"Just for spite I'll go."

The meeting was held in the basement of an apartment house down in the Village. It had not yet started when Herb and Dorothy came in. There was a big crowd and all the seats were taken. A lot of talk and a lot of smoke filled the large room. They were having a little trouble with the movie projector and a crowd of young men were clustered about the operator, offering suggestions. Very old men and very young men without beards and without long hair, girls without horn-rimmed spectacles and braided long hair, elderly women without pinched noses and stringy arms, thin lips, were talking and arguing and laughing.

Dorothy led Herb over to where a group was having a lot of fun. The men were between twenty-five and fifty, and the women were younger. One of the girls said, "I thought you weren't coming."

"Oh, I wanted to bring this right-wing Hitlerite up here so we could beat his brains out and tar and feather him."

They grinned at Herb and waited for him to say something.

"She has me down wrong," he said. "I'm a left-wing DAR. I belong to the William Randolph Hearst League for the Preservation of Bolshevism in the United. States and I'm boosting Mayor Hague as chief organizer for the Communist Party."

"He'd make a good organizer for the Communists," said a thickly built garment worker. "They want guys like him."

"In your hat," a girl snapped back at him. She was a hosiery worker. "You Lovestonites could use him better than we could."

"Are you a member of the party?" someone asked Herb.

"Don't let them get started with you, Herb." Dorothy pushed the last speaker in the chest. "You leave him alone," she said. "If you get him all mixed up the first thing we know he'll be over in Madrid spying for Franco."

They stood there joking until the meeting started. There was an American flag to one side of the small platform, on which ten people sat in comfortable positions. The audience quieted down quickly and the first speaker got up and talked for ten minutes. He concluded by asking for volunteers to solicit funds for another Loyalist ambulance. There were twenty-five volunteers. Dorothy was one of them. Then a girl about twenty-four took the platform and discussed the Japanese boycott drive. This was followed by a half-hour talk by an elderly man who spoke about Nazi activities in the United States. After him the returned volunteers from Spain were introduced.

The first was a young man, in his early twenties. Before he had gone over to Spain his hair had been glinting red. "Look at his hair now," Dorothy whispered to Herb. She had known the boy well. The boy's hair was now more gray than red. He had trouble with his speech. Once he stopped for almost a half-minute trying to get a word out. He was discussing the problem of Loyalist propaganda in democratic nations. He was extremely incoherent and it was a job to sit there and listen to him. But the audience sat back and listened attentively and tried to give him the impression that he was doing very well as far as they were concerned. He finished his talk and was well applauded.

"What's wrong with him?" said Herb.

"Shell-shocked." Dorothy pointed. "See how he walks, how his— notice? He's not sure of himself at all."

The other volunteers gave short speeches. Three of them had been shell-shocked. There was one who was still taking treatments after having been hospitalized in Spain for nine months with an explosive bullet wound in his left shoulder moving down and coming out of his back in a wide gap that still drained pus. There was another with superficial wounds across his chest and stomach and a deep bayonet gash in his right arm.

They spoke about political theories and propaganda methods and problems of financing various projects. None of them spoke about battle experiences.

One of them was very interesting. Dorothy said that she had never seen or heard of this man before, but she would really like to meet him after the meeting was over. He was about forty. He had been wounded twice. The second time he had been given up for dead. But after a Loyalist advance he was picked up and they took three bullets from his body.

He was speaking about his sentiments in regard to the war. He was summing up the situation as he saw it.

"... you want to stop this thing. It's not worth the price. Now that sounds like treason. I don't care if it is treason, although I assure you that it isn't. It's not worth the price. There are values higher than the mere difference between political theories. The soldiers in the trenches are suffering, but the women and children, the innocents, are still being blown to bits and starved and thrown out of their homes into actual battle areas. Sure, we're in the right. I say that and I believe it. But on the other side one of their men is giving a speech now and he says that they are in the right. That's why we're fighting. We both believe that we're in the right. And because we're fighting to defend our beliefs, women and children are being killed. We ought to stop it ..."

"How can you stop it!" someone cried from the audience.

"Please reserve your questions until the speaker has finished," the chairman said.

The man who was speaking went on, "We ought to stop it, that's what I said. When you ask me how we can stop it, I don't have to fish for facts or figures. We can stop it by cooperation among all interested groups, to continue a fight for peace. And peace will come only when we overthrow the forces primarily responsible for the tragedy that is taking place in Spain today!"

"He's a pretty clever speaker," said Herb. "I bet I know what he'll say next."

"The factors of fascism and Nazism must be downed in a worldwide drive. Unless that is done the Spanish Civil War will continue indefinitely. Because it is no longer—"

He went on in this vein and repeated himself many times. He stumbled over a few sentences and at the finish he answered questions very poorly. After the meeting Dorothy went up to him and asked him why the whole tone of his speech had changed so suddenly.

"You were saying that you wanted it stopped," she said. "I was expecting you to go on and ask for a surrender, or at least the beginning of peace terms. Weren't you going to do that? Didn't something stop you?"

"Yes," he said, "when that fellow yelled out and asked me how could we stop it, I lost the entire theme of my talk. Or rather, I wanted to lose it. That's the way it is. One minute I wanted to ask for peace and the next minute I was yelling all over again for a stronger renewal of the fight against fascism. There are so many confusing issues, aren't there?"

"Yes, we're—"

"We're dazed," he said.

"But we mustn't be."

He looked at her with an expression of sadness that suddenly changed to one of determination. "You're right," he said, "we mustn't be."

After that Dorothy was very quiet and when she and Herb were invited to a party after the meeting she said that she was very tired. Driving back she had very little to say, and Herb was quiet also.

They said good night very briefly and she told him to come up the following night. She stayed awake most of the night, thinking about Tommy and what he was fighting for. Dorothy fell asleep telling herself that she should not think about it too much.

CHAPTER VIII

From his bed Tommy could look to one side out of the window which had once held stained glass, but which was now open, and which showed him the sky. He was on his back, in this church made into a hospital. The nurses worked hard, because there were many wounded here, and there was much moving and work going on all day long.

Tommy would be here another week. And then he would rest for two weeks before going back to the front. For a while it had looked serious. He had lost much blood, and that first night he had been very bad. But he was strong, his resistance was good, he rested here now and felt comfortable.

It looked nice outside. If he was back home he would be at work now, and he would not be able to see the sky. In the factory it was dark and noisy, it was a well of dust from wood and steel, it lasted too long each day. Now he could rest here and take it easy. He shifted slightly to one side.

There comes a time when a single hope, repeated too often, becomes a painful stab. The first few months had been bad enough. And after that each time he thought of Dorothy was in itself a wistful, gentle wish that she could be with him. Following, there were the minutes and hours of almost maddening need for her. Now, looking out at the sky through the church window, the thought of her came floating at him, and he sensed it as a grinding, somewhat leering outward force, telling him that here he was, unable to see her. She was too far away.

But then another thought was striking him with even greater pain. He had not mailed that letter. He had not written a letter. Oh, yes, he had. Yes, sure, in the trench right before the attack. No, he had torn it up. Yes, he had torn it, and now it was three weeks, and she had received no letter from him. He had to write a letter.

The last one he had received from her was beneath his pillow. He reached for it and looked over some of the paragraphs. Through the wisecracks and the funny people that she had seen and made up out of her own ideas, and through the nonsense, the ridiculous things written down there, he could see her sitting alone and writing with tears in her eyes, sobbing while thinking of things to make him laugh.

Booming, then cracking, booming again and flattening out to a dull consistent murmur, the noise of the front reached him. He looked straight ahead, holding Dorothy's letter and listening, while the guns worked. A definite impatience charged in upon him. He wanted to get out of here and get up there and fight. A less definite impatience followed. He wanted this war to be won and done with, and he wanted to get back to Dorothy.

The guns boomed and cracked.

CHAPTER IX

It was raining. When the rain came down she liked to sit and read. Either that or be watching a movie. If people were around she was uncomfortable. If one person was around her when it was raining, particularly a heavy rain like that which was bursting now, she could not sit still or talk reasonably.

But if she was alone when it was raining, then there was comfort and she could just sit still and read. Maybe her thoughts would not center on the page before her. She might be thinking of something else, like now, sitting there with a magazine on her lap, looking at the page before her, which was gray print broken off at one side by a blue and orange scene showing a man standing in deep thought beside a weeping woman.

Jean looked at the page but her thoughts centered upon George Green, who had called up five minutes ago. She had not spoken very kindly to him and he had hung up somewhat furiously and had said that he would not see her today, nor tonight, perhaps not the rest of this week anyway. It was Wednesday now. That meant he would not see her until Sunday.

It was three weeks today that he had started that fight with Herb. It was four weeks, or was it five, since she had last been alone with Paul. Should she call Paul up now? She looked outside and it was raining very hard. Her eyes took in the page and the blue and orange picture.

Suppose one of these days Paul should come charging into the room yelling that he could not stand it any longer, that she should pack her things and they would go away together. He would come running in, his heavy strong body vibrant and charged with a current of rebellion against all that which had held him back for so long. She pictured this. She let it go a little further and she saw him picking her up and carrying her bodily out of the room.

Her mind went back to the night when she had been alone with him in this very room, on this very couch, a night when Wilda was away over the weekend visiting her brother in Columbus, and Herb was at an advertising banquet at one of the big hotels. She had called up, and Paul was home alone. She had casually asked him to come over, she did not want to stay alone. He did not want to come. But she had coaxed.

After he was in the room with her for a while, and their conversation was somewhat forced, they stopped talking. She sat down on the sofa and he monkeyed around with the radio. She put her feet up on the sofa. He turned the radio off and then she was lying on the sofa looking at him. He slowly came over, stopped once, and then gave in. He came over to the sofa.

There is no one like Paul, she said to herself. The body of a man, not tall, in fact short, as short as Herb, but broad and tough, hard like the trunk of a great tree. His skin, face, hands, the feeling of him, his hair, the color of his skin and the color of his eyes. His voice. Him. Paul. Come here, Paul, come here to me.

What made you remember things? Certain things. What brought them to your mind and kept them there? Certain things caused certain things. Had it really been all right that night with Paul? Was it all right now?

No. Of course it was not all right. That was why she was thinking about it now. That was how things were. If it had been all right it would have been forgotten, but now suddenly things were happening inside her and that was why she was thinking about Paul.

It was happening then that she was having a baby. Forming inside her. This was life coming to be existent inside her, a process of creation taking place because of a certain night with Paul. That was it. She was having a baby.

Greatly thrilled, Jean rushed to the phone and made an appointment with her doctor for that evening. And then she went back to the magazine. It was raining very hard.

Of course, she was having Paul's baby.

What would he say? Would he say that it was not true, that they had both taken care? Would he say that it was really absurd, that Herb had more to do with it than he? She started to laugh. Herb. She thought of the nights in bed with Herb, pushing him away, saying no no no, shaking her head and pushing him away. She did not think of two or three nights when she had not said no, when she had felt like it and had cooperated very well with Herb.

The doctor said that she was indeed having a baby. She made another appointment with him and then went back to the apartment. She had not been there ten minutes when the bell rang and George Green was down in the lobby. She said that he could come up if he wanted to.

George still had a slightly swollen nose. He was dressed in a very heavy tweed suit that made her warm just to look at him. The rain had stopped and the breeze following the rain had died down. Now it was very warm. The windows were open but it was getting hot and here George was facing her with a thick tweed suit on and an oxford shirt with thick knitted tie and sweat running down his face.

"I couldn't stay away, Jean. I know you don't want to see me for some reason but I had to come over."

"Sit down, George. Don't stand there like a soldier."

"Don't you really want to see me, Jean?"

"Please stop acting like a college boy. It's tiresome listening to you. Like one of those roast beef and ale love stories with an Oxford background and plenty of suppressed tears."

"Where did you get that one?" he said. When she tried to imitate somebody she almost always ruined the works.

But she came back at him fast and her voice was keen. "I'm in no mood to have any kind of a scene with you right now, George. If you want to sit still and be nice, all right. If you feel like kissing me, I suppose I won't object too much. But I refuse to argue with you on any point whatever."

"Oh, you do."

"Maybe you better go, after all, George. I don't like you today."

"Oh, you don't."

"Oh, you do, oh, you don't. You're absolutely boring, do you realize that?"

"There's been times when I wasn't so boring."

"And there'll be other times too. But you've got to behave yourself and keep your voice down and not be nasty."

"All right, Mrs. Hervey." He did not have the right kind of a face for a thin smile, but the one he was putting on now wasn't bad. It showed something about him that she had faintly suspected, but had never really thought about. Now he was smiling in this thin way, and he was bent forward slightly to see how she would take it.

Jean nearly fell. She drew in a great breath which tore at her and finally came out in a rush of words so fast that she did not know what she was saying. "You cheap dirty welsher, this is a new technique, isn't it! It's a fine way to start a loan fund without having to pay interest and without having to pay principal. Well, let me get one thing understood here, George Green. Oh, pardon me, E. George Green, the pride and joy of every law office in town as long as he stays good and far away—listen to me, youngster, you get in a huddle with yourself and call it a bad day, because you're not playing around with a lovable old darling who's going to keep you in lollipops and ice-cream sodas. We had a few very nice times together and it was all right as long as you behaved yourself. But as soon as our young-man-about-town begins getting ideas about high finance, it's time to have a showdown—"

"That's what I'm here for, a showdown."

There was something peculiarly merciless about his tone, and the way he was standing there and studying her. "Explain yourself," she said.

"Sure. I need money. You're going to give me some. If you don't I have ways and means of telling people just what kind of life you and your husband are leading, and I—"

Jean laughed. She enjoyed this part of it. "And you call yourself a lawyer. If you had half the brains I originally gave you credit for, and incidentally, that wasn't too much anyway, you'd know that neither I nor my husband care what you say, because anything you'd say would hurt you more than us."

"What makes you so sure of that?"

"Oh, cut it out. You've said too much already and you've turned out to be one of the most ignorant men Eve ever come up against, and also the cheapest."

His expression changed. He suddenly realized that he had made a fool of himself in these last two minutes and that he had played a trick on no one but himself. If he had gone about this differently he might have gotten a few much needed dollars off her and he could try again tomorrow with the dice. He was due for a win and all he needed was the dough to put down on the table. Now he had messed things up properly. The situation had called for a delicately worked pass over the center of the line and instead he had tried a clumsy buck through guard. He stared dully at Jean, and lowered his head slightly.

"You can't get away with this sort of thing," he mumbled.

"Oh, please get out and stop bothering me," she said.

She turned her back on him and walked into the bedroom. George tightened his lips and curled one over his lower teeth, pressing it with the upper.

He followed Jean into the bedroom.

"You caused me a lot of trouble," he said. Indirectly, she had. With Jean it was not simply a case of spending a night with her and forgetting about it, then casually meeting her again in a month or so, and spending another night with her. Jean had a grip that kept on tightening even after a man thought it was broken. George had borrowed heavily and had lost at the gambling tables. If someone asked him now why he had done this, he would not be able to explain. But he had wanted money badly. He wanted to buy her things and to take her places. Perhaps he really wanted to take her away with him. Right now he could not say just what he had planned.

But he had made quite a few plans and now they were blown to bits. He was standing here like a big dumb lug and she was telling him in a tired, bored voice that she wanted him to leave.

"It really is a shame about you," she said.

He moved nearer her. "You must do this quite a lot. I bet you get a lot of fun out of it, don't you? Pick up some guy on the street and give him the sweetest little runaround that he ever had, and then tell him that it's a shame about him."

"If you remember correctly," she said, not even looking his way, "I never asked to meet you. You were more or less responsible for our sudden coming together. And you carried it off pretty nicely, even if it did have a little too much of the campus about it."

"Yeah, I was just a poor misunderstood boy and you figured you'd give me a break."

"More or less."

He was still coming closer to her. Very slowly he moved within reach of her and when she turned her head she could see that he was coming for her. She wondered for an instant why he was moving like this, toward her. Then she looked into his eyes and she started back. He reached out and took her wrist.

"Let me go! What are you—"

George attempted to control himself here. He held his fist back. It was parallel with his shoulder. He tried to let it drop to his side. But instead it went forward and hit Jean on the jaw. She was knocked unconscious.

A man goes to college and for three years he is a big man around the campus. He plays football hard and likes to play it because he does well at it. He is big and hard, he likes physical encounter, and he does very well on the field. He is really not ignorant and he is not too lazy. Furthermore he realizes the prestige of being known as a man with both brains and athletic ability. He does fairly well in his classes and he is not going to a country club. He is going to a school with a reputation.

When he gets out, therefore, he is fairly well known. He is George Green and by this time he is twenty-four. It is not difficult for him to get into Princeton Law School, and after he gets in he sees that things are going to be different from now on. He gets around. He goes to big parties and dances. He meets sons of important families. He makes his connections, because he realizes that three years are going to pass very swiftly, and he must do a lot of high-pressure sales work while he is here at law school.

But there is no football team at law school. It is hard work and there is a serious aspect to it that increases in alarming proportions as the first year gives way to the second and the second gives way to the third.

If a man comes from a wealthy family, if his father is a big lawyer, if his uncle is a big lawyer, it is something different. He feels high through every day of those three years because he sees himself in the office after he gets out and his name is on the door practically as soon as he passes his examinations.

George Green, however, did not come from a wealthy family. His father had very little money to begin with, and now he was making less and less. Things looked very dark.

Furthermore, George Green could not hold friends very long. He had really found this out in his last year at Princeton. Up to that time he had figured that he was the one who let the other fellow go. But in that final term a few unpleasant things had happened, a few remarks had been made, there was one fist fight that had not lasted very long, and there were some very significant actions on the part of men whom he had once thought liked him.

Now he was in New York City and it was the beginning of July. He was walking away from an apartment house where he had clipped Jean Hervey in the jaw. She was probably still out. He was on this street now, walking away while she was unconscious on her bedroom floor.

He had just knocked out a woman with a punch in the jaw. He had no job. He had two dollars in his pocket. There were a lot of addresses in the little book in his pocket. He wondered where to go first. He took out the book and while he looked at the names moving up and down before his eyes, he felt his hands shaking.

"I'll find something, before long I'll find something and then I'll spit in everybody's face."

But right now he was going toward his room. He was going up the stairs. That meant he wasn't on the street anymore. He was going upstairs to his room. Then he was sitting at the table and thinking about a sweet quiet girl who had really liked him when he was at North Carolina. Besides this sweet quiet kid there were the dances every Saturday night, there were the nights of intelligent card playing and bull sessions in the fraternity house, the excursions around the vicinity looking for trouble, then summer, mellow, languid summers taking it easy and waiting for the first day of training for football. Sweat and leather, braces and supporters, heaving low, coming up hard and into the tackling dummies, the charging machines on which stood the coach being pushed around, yelling to get lower, to bring the shoulders into it with a powerful lift of the torso. The days passing like this, moving into fall, which was still hot, but which was comfortably hot in the stadium with everyone shouting, the ball in the air, the new cleats sure and ready on the firm green turf.

That sweet quiet kid, not saying much and liking him so very much. She was probably married to some doctor down there now, living in a quiet little white house in a quiet little town, leading a quiet life.

Well, he wanted something like that. It was really nothing to run away from. Now that he thought of it, he had never been uncomfortable or sulky, or in any kind of bad humor when that kid had been around. She was pretty, she was not exciting, but she could probably learn how to thrill after a little while. Some of those kisses had really been sweet. But it was past now. It might have been yesterday, but even if it was, it was still past.

Tomorrow he would have to begin around ten. Seven full hours of looking for a job. Then at the end of a day like that, he would feel that at least he had been doing something. And then again, he would have to get money somehow. An idea came to him. He would call up this Jean tomorrow and apologize, put on a real act and ask her if he could see her again. Sometimes a sock in the jaw meant a lot to a woman. At times it meant more than a kiss. It might mean an awful lot to Jean. He would call up tomorrow and see how things would work out.

And in the meantime there would probably be a few bucks from the old man in the morning mail. That would let him eat for a few days. He sighed slightly and went out of the room. He walked downstairs and outside. It was raining again. He put up his coat collar and walked three blocks to a small restaurant where he bought a bowl of vegetable soup, two ham sandwiches, two cups of coffee and a plate of ice cream. He bought a pack of cigarettes and smoked in the doorway of the restaurant, waiting for the rain to stop. It was raining very hard now.

Jean sensed that she was lying down. She sensed a pain in her jaw. Her eyes were closed. She opened them. She was on the floor of her bedroom and she was alone. Her jaw hurt very much and that was because she had been hit there. She got to her feet very slowly and as she did this the fist was crashing into her jaw again and knocking her down. She stared into the mirror and nearly fainted again when she saw her jaw. It was swollen and her mouth looked crooked.

In some way she must get back at him. The chances were that she would never see this George Green again, but if she ever did come across him, she was going to get back at him. The only way to make a man like that suffer was not to take anything away from him, or hurt him physically, or insult him. George could be made miserable only by decreasing him in his own estimation. And that would be a job, she reflected.

These matters, however, did not bother her very much. It was her jaw that bothered her. It hurt very much and it looked bad. She went into the kitchen and put some ice to it.

While Jean was occupied pressing ice against her jaw, something else was taking place inside her. It slowly started to hurt and then it made her dizzy. At first she thought it was her jaw again. But then she sensed the pain and she gave a little frightened shriek and darted out of the kitchen into the parlor. She told herself that she was going to faint and she whirled, and more or less voluntarily fell on the sofa. The pain was really not very bad, she told herself now, but she was still dizzy, as if she had been inhaling too much strong smoke, and she took the telephone off the receiver and called the Schuens.

Wilda answered the phone and Jean claimed that she was very sick. Would Wilda please be the dearest darling in the whole world and come over with Paul? It was really nothing more than a bad stomach, probably made worse by a case of the blues. Wilda was very sympathetic but said that she was feeling none too well herself today. She would send Paul over to cheer Jean up.

Jean got dressed and kept holding an icebag against her jaw. She timed herself while she stood before the mirror fixing her hair and putting stuff on her face. Paul would be over in ten minutes. She would have to be suffering in bed when he came in. Her hair would be half over her face, on one cheek. No, better still she would be lying on her back, her eyes closed when he came in. In bed, she pressed the icebag hard against her face and waited.

"You're sure now?"
"Of course I'm sure. I told you what the doctor said."
"Maybe we can do something."
"What do you mean, Paul?"
"I mean—"
"We can't do anything, Paul."
"I guess we can't. But—say look, Jean, I—I want to be—well, I

want to be sure of this. I—don't you think I have a right to be—well, sure of it? You know, it's—"

"Aren't you sure of it now? Don't you believe me?"

"Yes." Do I? Do I?

"Don't look that way, Paul. I don't feel bad about it. I don't think I've ever been happier. I said to myself before you came in, I'm bearing Paul a child, and that is how it should be, because I love him, and he loves me, and now we're having a child, and—"

"What about Herb?"

"Herb?"

"Yes, Herb. And Wilda? What about them?"

"Right now I'm not thinking about Herb and Wilda. I'm thinking about you and me, and our baby."

Her eyes were filmed now with a luster that thickened and then receded, so that the light of the room was reflected in them like star beams upon a dark pool. And her lips parted slightly, her arms came out from beneath the cover and went up to him. As always he was lost, bewildered, and then completely overwhelmed, like a helpless swimmer in a rip tide, taken out slowly, stunned by the bounding breakers, then pulled out with ever increasing swiftness until the tide slackened and there was nothing more but the depths beneath, the surrender, a clutching arm slowly covered by the water.

CHAPTER X

In a big city, the heat seems to collect itself together and strike at those spots where the people are jammed up close against one another and there is plenty of sweat, plenty of headaches, and plenty of weariness. This heat seems to bash down upon the heads of people working hard side by side in factories, in warehouses, and also in offices.

It is as hard upon office workers as it is upon laborers, perhaps harder. Because in the summertime there are days when there is nothing to do in an office except sit at a desk with the pants or dress sticking to the wood varnish, and tell the self how hot it is outside and in here. There is a lot of drinking cold water, and much mopping of brows, besides a weary drone of conversation based on the weather and prospects for a cool evening.

This first week in July was very hot. It was also a very busy week for Herb. The agency had handled three new accounts with a great deal of success, and the advance in reputation meant an increase in business. It was a rush week. It was such a busy week that the entire force went at it with a zeal hitherto seldom noticed by the higher-ups.

The result was that on Saturday morning there was little or nothing to do. Much work had been cleared up and everyone went around looking for more to do but the work was already done. There were a few details that could be looked into, but these could be left for another day if necessary.

Herb sat at his desk and put some papers to one side. Tonight he would go up to see Dorothy and they would go out together. They would eat and drink and hear music, they would dance, they would go for a ride, laugh, yell, and she would put her arms around him and want him to love her because she was a woman who was so very much in love with a man that when he was far away and could not be with her, she had to express this by releasing her physical need on someone who was so very much like Tommy in so many ways that it was not hard to believe at times that he really was Tommy.

By this time Herb had the whole business down pat in his mind and there were moments when he caught himself thinking that he was a fool not to look at this in the same way as Dorothy. But these moments were as drops of water against an ocean when compared with the time he spent feeling satisfied, pure and decent because he had held back so long.

Yet at the same time Herb sensed that the practical side of the matter was resolving itself into a serious problem. Every time he left Dorothy there was a serious physical strain that got worse each time. He would have to do something about that because it was one thing to keep this relationship flowing along in beauty and purity, and it was quite another thing to take a last look at a body like Dorothy's that beckoned and gladly welcomed, then to turn around and go to a room and sleep alone.

He knew himself well enough to realize that this could go so far and no further. He would have to keep on seeing Dorothy and he would have to keep himself from taking her in his arms. But he had to have physical satisfaction and he was trying to think of an address not far from the apartment, when Miss Gillen came into the office.

This Gillen girl was thirty years old, and she looked it. She worked hard, she ate well, she lived in a clean bright room with another woman a few years younger than herself. There had been several boyfriends and there had been very many enjoyable evenings in that room. But both Gillen and the other girl were quite particular, and although they were quite normal and capable of handling the situation, they mutually realized the importance of careful selection and moderation. Not very interested in marrying, they were contented and did not go to many pains to attract men. Miss Gillen herself had the natural advantages of a straight, even posture, and a good digestion. She had very clean habits and even in hot weather she kept herself pleasant by taking two showers a day and putting a certain cream under her armpits. On her dresser there was a bottle of extremely expensive perfume, and she used this so sparingly that its faintness was perhaps her greatest attraction.

"I took those papers down to Mr. Edwinns, and he said that he'll look them over and he wants you to come down to see him before you go out."

"Did you look up that last copy we did for Connart Lace? The one we—"

"Yes, but Mr. Edwinns called up that he wanted to see it so I took that down to him with the others."

"That's good. Now if a mistake is made he can't say that he didn't see it before I did. It might be a good idea for you to do that in the future, Miss Gillen. I don't think Mr. Edwinns is particularly overworked right now, and it would make all three of us happier if he took on a few more responsibilities, don't you think?"

"Yes, I do. There really isn't anything wrong in it."

"There really isn't anything wrong in a lot of things if you look at them sensibly."

"No, and—Mr. Hervey, you've got your hand on my leg."

"I realize that."

He put his other hand up and moved his chair back from the desk. She sat down easily in his lap and they kissed each other simply. They looked at each other and did not smile. Miss Gillen took a deep breath that made her look very refreshing and sincere in that instant and Herb rested back in the chair as she pressed slightly more against him.

They kissed again, not too long, very simply, and Miss Gillen put her hand on his cheek and then ran it up through his hair and back over his neck and across his ear, onto his cheek again. They were looking at each other without blinking and then Herb moved back even more in the chair. Miss Gillen moved back with him and put her lips on his softly and easily. They were both very comfortable. In the other offices the men and women groaned in the heat.

"There was one more thing I wanted to tell you," he said. "If we get the proofs of the Rayburn matter in by Monday, you take those down to Mr. Edwinns, if you don't mind. Just say that Mr. Hervey figured he'd like to see them first. Because if you bring them in to me, I might begin making changes right away and then Edwinns will go back and ruin things as usual."

"I see what you mean. All right."

"What time is it? Look at my wrist."

"It's twelve, a minute of."

"Would you have lunch with me, please?"

"Certainly."

She got up from his lap and arranged her hair and dress, taking her time, and he pushed the chair back. She went to the door and said, "I'll see you downstairs."

"Yes, I'll be right out."

It was very satisfying to walk next to this Miss Gillen. She was about an inch shorter than he and she did not bump into him, or veer away from him. When she walked, she walked straight ahead and did not get out of anybody's way.

While they ate, their talk came easily, although neither talked too much. He looked across the table because he really wanted to get a good look at her. Herb could not get over the fact that he had been working in the same office with this for three years without ever looking into the situation and seeing what could be done about it.

In the big cool restaurant they sat and smoked.

Then they walked slowly toward the subway, which she had to take now, and he asked her if they couldn't meet tomorrow afternoon and perhaps go to one of the beaches.

"That would be fine," she said.

Herb watched her as she went down the subway steps.

With Dorothy that night he began by remaining very quiet. She asked him if anything was wrong, and he replied that on the contrary he felt better now than he had for a long time. She kept prodding him to find out just why this change had occurred, and the most she could get out of him was that his health and business and general outlook were very good now.

But as the evening passed, he forgot everything as always when he was with Dorothy for more than an hour at a time, and he began to look at her, think about her, think about her more deeply as she talked to him.

Again she wanted him to stay with her. She said that he was very annoying, very mean and disgustingly inconsiderate. He kissed her forehead and said good night. As he went back to his room, driving slowly through the thick black band that wound down through the dark city, he leaned comfortably against the velour and looked up at the heavy sky. It would be extremely hot tomorrow. Idly he wondered if Miss Gillen could also swim well.

It turned out that she could. She wore a skirted bathing suit that was conservatively stylish. When she entered the water and dove neatly through the first wave, she looked very sure of herself, and he could see that she enjoyed it. He swam out after her. They went out far and then whirled about, trod water and looked back at the beach.

"Nice."

"It's very clean out here. I like to swim out far for that reason. I hate the crowds in the shallow water," she said. "I wonder how deep it is."

"Surface dive. You know how to do that?"

"Sure." He breast-stroked twice and then turned over. He went too far over but nevertheless had enough force to go down far. When he came up he passed right next to her. He put his arms around her and she did the same to him.

Miss Gillen had the type of face that looks very attractive in a tight bathing cap. And when the water passed over her head, gleaming on the light green rubber cap, and gleaming on her smooth healthy skin, she made a smart picture.

"Do you like your work in the office?" he said.

"I don't mind it. At times it's interesting, but some days I must admit I watch the clock. Do you?"

"Yes, a lot."

"I thought so. You're—"

"Well?"

"You're really not fitted for that work, I've often thought."

"Oh no?" His lips formed a thin smile. "Why not?"

"Well, you're imprisoned in there, I think. Maybe you don't know it yourself, but that's the impression I get from you. You like a lot of room, don't you?"

"Why do you say that?"

"You're restless."

"Maybe. I don't know." He looked at her intently. She took his hands and put them behind her. They treaded water in slow rhythm.

"Look out there," she said.

Together they stared out at the horizon. This day was extremely hot and the sun glaring down on the water made it green dotted gold. It faded out indistinctly, calm all the way out to the haze beneath gray-yellow sky.

"Would you like to swim out there, keep on going until you couldn't go any further and then sink?"

"Not right now I wouldn't," he said.

"Tell me why?"

"Because I don't see any good reason to swim out there and drown myself. On the other hand, I see a few very good reasons why I should go on living."

"What are they?"

"That I don't know either. But they're there. If they weren't, I guess maybe I'd feel it somehow. Everybody has that feeling. Don't you? You don't want to swim out there and sink, do you?"

"No. Oh, definitely not." He took his hands away, but she reached back and put them there again. She pressed them there.

In a little while she said that she would like to lie on the beach and get some sun. They began to swim slowly back toward shore.

They took a room for the night at this place. They went to a cabaret and there was a good orchestra there and a very good show. She danced well and after a duckling, the orange cordial made her extremely witty and really amusing. They stayed up very late and yet they were not too tired when they came into the room.

After he put out the light they stood at the open window for a few minutes looking out at the white sand surface edging into the blackness of water and sky, broken only by thin, restless lines of foam. The salt wind cut through a hot stillness and pushed against their faces like a smooth wall of cool metal.

Miss Gillen did not need an alarm clock. She awoke at the same time each morning as if stirred by an automatic signal. Now as gray light bounded through the window she sat up in bed and stretched, then looked down with friendly eyes on Herb. She kissed his cheek and he opened his eyes and looked up at her. They kissed and she said, "If we hurry up we can take a dip before we drive back to town."

They quickly put on their bathing suits and ran out onto the beach. The water was cold but they stayed in for only a minute and then they went back to the hotel and dressed slowly because they had plenty of time. They went into the restaurant with salt-water-inspired appetites and ate big breakfasts.

The car zoomed along the road, eating up the miles in almost a straight line back to town. There was practically no traffic until they hit the city. He left her off at the office and then he parked the car.

He came into the outer office and two of the five girls were already at their desks, typing. Some of the men were gathered at a desk, looking over copy.

"Good morning."

"Good morning, Mr. Hervey."

"Good morning, Miss Gillen."

"Good morning, Mr. Hervey."

It was going to be a very busy day but he welcomed the work because he felt fine and now he was sitting down to his desk and his mind was clear, he was taking papers from the wire tray and in a few minutes he was deep in the network of a problem in advertising. He solved it thoroughly and went onto the next. The day passed quickly and he accomplished much. Before he left the office he figured that just for fun he would call up Jean and exchange a few words on things in general, perhaps find out what her immediate plans were in regard to the apartment. The hotel room was not exactly uncomfortable but after all it was his apartment and it was quite luxurious. He was already dialing the number when he figured he would put it off for a few days. Right now he did not feel like arguing with her anyway.

CHAPTER XI

Go get yourself into a mess but it's really not a mess. In some ways it's exciting and in some ways it's sweet. In many ways it's sweet. At any rate it's satisfying. When, you analyze it, it's really not a mess. The only miserable aspect to this is that he doesn't feel like I do although he will come around to it. I must be very nice to him and agree with him on oh, so many things. But he must come to see things my way. Why do I love him so much? And I really do love him. Why so much?

Paul came in and Jean was waiting for him at the door. She softly came close to him but drew away when she saw how his brows were brought together in a troubled and suffering strain.

"How do you feel?"

"Oh, fine, darling."

"No pain yet?"

"Oh, Paul, there's no pain for a long time yet."

"You look all right."

"Do I, Paul?"

"Yes, you look beautiful. I've never seen you looking like this before."

"Oh, then up to now you never thought I was beautiful."

"I've always thought so. But I've never seen you looking like this before."

He took her hands and tried to force a smile past his troubled features. It came slowly, and Jean said, "You're very worried, aren't you?"

He nodded and she murmured, "Why?"

"Well, Gehrig isn't hitting like he should be and even the pitching is falling down. The team looks shot."

"That's right. Grin like that. Joke. I want you to."

The phone rang. At the other end of the wire George Green was begging her to let him come over. He was talking very fast, and she listened dully and tried to piece together the jigsaw puzzle of what he was saying. Something about being so sorry and thinking about it all the time, and wanting so very much to see her. Before she could say why, she told him that it would be all right for him to come over.

When he arrived, Jean and Paul were in the midst of a forced conversation on the matter of what they should do about Wilda and Herb. Paul had been doing most of the talking, and he had been repeating himself and making a general botch of the whole business, saying over and over again that he really did not know what they should do.

"Oh—I didn't know."

"It's quite all right. George, meet Mr. Schuen, Paul Schuen."

"Oh. Hello—"

"George Green, Paul, a friend of mine."

"How do you do?"

It was a bad two minutes for George. He wondered why this guy was here with her and why she had said it was all right for him to come up when she was already with another guy. And this other guy looked as if he knew what the score was, all right. He looked about forty, and he had a good-natured face that could also be hard and mean, but was probably always good-natured like this. He was nobody to start trouble with, thought George. And there would be no trouble. George was not out for trouble. He had started and suffered enough of that. Now he wanted to have a general calm prevail, and a renewal of his friendship with Jean. He had hoped to come over here and apologize for what he had done, then to begin all over again and see what could be accomplished in the matter of a little financial help. His resources by this time were at a desperately low ebb.

All right, there was only one thing to do now. He would have to get out of here fast and wait a little while. It was a tough situation.

"Sorry I intruded. I—I—was in the neighborhood—"

"Oh, that's all right, George. What was it you wanted to see me about?"

It was getting a little close. When it came to creating agony, this Jean did all right for herself. She was getting a big kick out of this. He wondered if this guy with her now wasn't a professional pug or roughneck brought up here for the express purpose of cutting a slice of black pudding for Jean. It was a probability.

"Nothing important."

Paul wondered why she had allowed this Green chap to come up. He did not realize that he was frowning and that he wanted to say something nasty. Behind all this there was something not within the rules.

Jean was purposely silent. Only when George backed toward the door and mumbled something about leaving did she say, "Oh, if you have something to say then say it. It's perfectly all right."

"Some other time." He looked at Paul.

"Oh, don't mind Paul," said Jean.

"Some other time." George turned and opened the door. "Sorry to be so—well, glad I met you—see you later, Jean."

"Wait a minute." Paul walked slowly forward. "What do you want with her?"

George stopped. "Huh?" He could either run fast down the steps or he could do what he was trying to keep himself from doing—clipping Jean in the jaw.

"The last time he was here, Paul, he knocked me unconscious."

"Now wait a minute—" George breathed like a runner now.

"What did he do?"

"He tried to blackmail me, and when he saw that it wouldn't work, he punched me and ran out while I was unconscious on the floor."

Paul said, "When was this?"

"The same day I called you up to tell you about myself—"

George could either apologize now and explain that this was why he had come over. Or he could do what he wanted to do very much, and that was to release the rage that bounced around within him now, leaping high and to the sides, growing as his fists clenched more tightly.

Paul stared at George. "Get out of here."

"I was going."

"Get out."

George looked at Jean. It looked as if she was smiling. He stared back at Paul. "What will you do if I don't get out?"

"Go in the other room, Jean."

She walked backwards slowly. She saw George look a challenge at Paul, she saw Paul move quickly to the side and close the door.

Then Paul was taking off his coat and George was taking off his. They came together, short hard punches, a tussle, Paul throwing George to one side, George coming in low and shooting his arms out like spears, his fists banging against Paul's face.

"Maybe you shouldn't have started this, old-timer," said George. "It won't do you any good."

Paul came forward, his face expressionless. George got under his guard again and slammed him in the mouth. But Paul still came on. George had to give way. He was moving back when he came in contact with a chair. He leaped to one side and hit Paul again. He moved away and said, "The last time I had trouble here I got the worst of it, didn't I, Jean?" He laughed, as if that last time would be the only time.

Then Paul was rushing at him and pinning him in a bear hug before he could get away. Paul was throwing him over his hip and then falling on him, picking him up and hooking a right to the jaw, getting in close with short hammer blows to the stomach, after each of which George grunted like a sick bull, and then an overhand, downward smash that hit George between the eyes, put him to his knees. Paul reached down and brought him up again, and then drew back his right arm and let George have it in the teeth. This sent him across the room, and he landed with a hard thud on his back. He was not out, but he remained there staring up at Paul, his arms outspread on the rug.

"Are you getting up?" said Paul.

George could not reply. Three teeth were floating around in the blood in his mouth, which was puffed out as if he had mush in there.

Paul went into the bedroom. Jean was packing things into a bag.

"What are you doing?"

"I'm packing. We're going away."

"No. Wait. We—well, that's the only thing we can do, isn't it?"

"Yes. You see that now, don't you?"

He nodded.

"You go back to your place and get your things together. Wilda's home now, isn't she?"

"Yes, Wilda's home now." He shook his head trying to get rid of the throbbing, the pumping going on in there.

"I'll call her up. She'll come over here and when she arrives I'll be gone. I'll write a note. We'll meet at that drugstore across from your garage in a half-hour. Then we'll go."

"We're running away, aren't we?"

She went into the other room and called up Wilda. She said that Paul had taken sick suddenly and they had called a doctor. She said that Paul was probably not seriously sick but it would be better for Wilda to come right over.

Jean hung up after hearing the receiver jammed down at the other end of the line. Paul left and Jean wrote a note to Wilda.

"Dear Wilda:
Paul and I are going away. It is something over which we have no control and we either had to do this or we couldn't live anymore. It got to a point where we had to decide one way or the other. Please try and understand. We don't know where we're going. We only know that because things are this way we've got to get away.
                                                           Jean."

She placed that note upright against the lamp on the table and then she picked up her bag. She moved toward the door but then stopped and went to the telephone and called up Herb at the office.

"You can come back to the apartment now," she said. "I'm going away."

"Have a nice time."

"Thanks."

"So long."

Jean stopped at the door and looked at George. He was watching her with wide eyes that would not blink. His face was pale and blood ran in several thick streams from his puffed lips. She turned away quickly and left.

The door was open for Wilda. She came in and saw the note. She read it and swayed. She saw George Green. She read the note again. And then again she looked at George Green. For a third time she read the note. Then she fainted.

George finally was able to get to his feet. He went to the bathroom and let the blood and teeth out of his mouth. He was barely able to move, and in a few minutes he was again so weak that he could only stagger to the sofa and fall heavily across it. Wilda regained her senses and read the note once more. She came over to George and knew that her voice sounded queer as she yelled, "When did they go, what do you know about it? Who are you? When—"

"I bet I know who you are," mumbled George, grinning like an idiot.

"Where did they go, where did they go—" She was shrieking now.

George groaned and turned over on the sofa, trying to bite into the upholstery. The plush touched his bleeding gums, and he groaned again. Wilda was talking to herself and dialing the telephone. She stopped before her number was received. She looked at the window.

Slowly she walked toward it and then stared down. Three stories beneath, the pavement was a white band and next to it was the street. It did not hurt. After you went out there was nothing until you hit the pavement. That only lasted a tenth of a second. Maybe you felt yourself break in two. But then it would be all over. She looked down.

On the sofa George twisted painfully and then heard the sound of Wilda's shoe scraping the wall beneath the window. He saw her getting up on the sill and he said, "What are you trying to do?" She was getting up there and he saw her from the side. He yelled, "Hey where you think you're going?" and he was able to fall to one side, recover himself, reach for her just as she was going out, and then pull her back toward him. They fell on the floor together and Wilda began to screech and kick.

He was ready to let her go and do whatever she wanted to, because he was hurt badly enough already and if one of her heels caught him in the face it would probably finish the job as far as his nose and teeth were concerned. He was still holding on to her, however, when there was a banging on the door and a little guy came in.

"Now we've been getting complaints about this apartment for the last—say, who are you—you don't belong here. Where's Mrs. Hervey—where's—"

George let go of Wilda and got to his feet. He hurried past the little guy and out of the apartment. The little guy whirled like a top and yelled for him to stop. But at that moment Wilda got to her feet and started for the window. The little guy yelled, "Help!" and jumped like a scared rabbit to one side. But then he took a hold on himself in the next instant and stopped Wilda as she again got her foot on the sill. He kept yelling, "Help! Help!" until some of the other tenants came running in and stopped the show. Someone called the police and someone else put smelling salts to Wilda's nose. Other tenants were piling into the room and there was a lot of noise that increased as one of the ladies got hold of Jean's note and one of the men saw blood on the floor. The little guy was going around in a frenzy trying to quiet them down and stop the excitement. But the news was getting around to the other rooms and everyone was having a grand time.

CHAPTER XII

Steadily the rebels came, pushing them back. They made several stands, their retreats were individual examples of superb military strategy, but to the south their defenses slackened. The motorized units were still moving up, the prods by the long, keen fingers of the rebel armies caught them at points of poor resistance. They were driven back.

Tommy Nicola could see the line advancing. He was in a village and the order had come an hour ago for the regiment to hold it as long as possible. This meant that they should simply hold it. Tommy looked out from his post on the second story of a shell-battered plaster dwelling. He had a two-weeks beard, there were small bloody wounds on his hands and arms, he coughed incessantly, and the lice, sweat and caked dirt were thick on his body. He looked out over the wall and saw them coming.

A man can last for so long and no longer. Tommy signaled to the major, who was also on the second story, and who also had his gun ready. They both took aim. Tommy got someone. They were coming on. They were running through the streets. The major got someone, and then jumped down from his post to see what was wrong with the machine guns on the first floor. The Loyalists woke up and began to shoot. It was not hard to hit the rebels, who had to come toward them along the narrow street. And the major was smart. He rushed thirty men across the street to another house. They also had a machine gun and they stopped the rebels, who left seventy men dead, and who made a temporary retreat and prepared a sudden rush. One of the tanks was made ready. There was a steady popping of rifle fire and the machine guns on both sides were working consistently but not doing much damage because everyone knew that he had to cover up.

Tommy could see five men very clearly and he took aim. But then he put the rifle down and decided to let it go. They really had a mob over there and no matter how low he ducked, they would know where he was, and they would get him just as sure as he was alive now.

But a man can last so long and no longer. When you've been in the thick of it for nearly two years, when you've been wounded three times, when you've had hand-to-hand fights in enemy trenches, in your own trenches, and when you've just about managed to come out of it each time, you come to realize that there must be a law of averages that will get you sooner or later.

He figured it out now. He didn't have anything else to do. He began to figure it out. Three times wounded, that is, seriously wounded. Or had that last time been serious? Yes, it had. And how many battles, how many bullets had passed near him? Within an area of five yards, how many bullets had passed by? Nearly two years. When would it be over?

Why couldn't they make one big push now, just decide to go on and keep on going and wipe them off the map? Could it really be done? Why didn't Miaja get them all together and bring them back like a slingshot and then release them in one big movement forward, with the tanks and the planes and everyone, going on like a flood to make this one big drive and win, win.

Yes, win it once and for all, stop it by winning it. That was the only way it could be stopped, by winning it. Win it then, and let him go back to Dorothy. A plane was coming. It wasn't a bird. It was a plane. There was another plane. Then another. Telegraph and radio were wonderful things. The rebels used airplanes wisely. Now these planes would come over and strafe them. Did the major see the planes? Tommy moved cautiously to one side, peeped through the wall and saw the major alone beneath the lower roof. Had he noticed the planes? Tommy knew that once seen, the men would not have a chance against those planes. These flyers would shoot down and keep on shooting, zooming up then coming down and strafing them some more until they would run out into the street. That would end it then and there. Had the major seen the planes yet?

Tommy could not move very fast. His left side was still quite stiff and he had a limp. But now he darted out from behind the wall and shouted to the major. There was a lot of noise and at first he was not heard. A bullet got him in the leg. The major saw him. Tommy shouted again and pointed. He fell down and crawled behind cover. The major had seen the planes before Tommy and when they came they had no one to pepper with bullets.

From the right, from the left, from center, reinforcements were coming up. The counterattack came swiftly and moved through the streets and fields with infantry fresh from the trucks at the outskirts of the town. Moving back, the rebels did not fight. They hurried back and left guns and a disabled tank behind.

When the stretcher bearers reached Tommy he closed his eyes and wondered how long the pain would last. The wound felt deep and there was a spreading feeling in his leg as if the bullet was still moving in there. The first-aid men lifted him gently onto the stretcher and the pain began as they took him down off the roof.

They were carrying him along the street and each step that they took seemed to spread the wound wider. They were nearing the ambulance now and just as they lifted him in, he fainted.

An explosive bullet had torn through Tommy's right leg. It bored through a little above the knee and nearly took the leg off. There was smashed bone and tissue there that was pulpy and soft. The blood was clogged and dark when they put him on the table, but the surgeon cut carefully and made a clean amputation without loss of much more blood. He took Tommy's leg off three and a half inches above the knee.

CHAPTER XIII

When the day was finished she could not remember one minute when she had not been thinking about him. In the factory it had been hot, the work had piled up and two girls had fainted. But now, looking back upon those hours, she smiled to think that the heat, the work, the time dragging on itself, had not bothered her. She had done more than any girl on the floor.

And all day long she had been thinking about him. She was remembering the day they had met, when a girlfriend had taken her to a meeting and someone had introduced an "exile from fascist Italy." Then Tommy had gotten up, without flourish, without violent speech, a young man of twenty-nine, tired physically after a hard day's manual labor, his body bent slightly as he stood at the rostrum.

Right now she could hear him again as he spoke evenly, interestingly, with a sincerity unadorned by loud phrases and wide gestures. Everything he did seemed to be just right. She was sitting there with her girlfriend and this girlfriend had leaned over and whispered, "Good-looking, isn't he?"

There was Tommy up there, not very tall, not very heavy, but strong. She could see that strength in his face, in his hands, the way he walked back to his chair.

Then afterwards, they had been introduced. He walked home with Dorothy and the girlfriend. He asked Dorothy if he could see her again. He called at her house. Her parents did not like the idea. But she was quite uninterested in what her parents liked or did not like. In two months they were married. Dorothy's father said that he would not help her one bit. He said that she was not reasonable and that he was very disappointed in her. She kissed him and told him not to worry too much about it. She kissed her mother and then said goodbye.

If it hadn't been Tommy, who would it have been? She thought of some of the specimens who had taken her out when she was at Wellesley. Their talk, their actions, their dress, and again their talk. Then there were some of the older ones who were now mooching and stooging and getting in with people, acting twelve hours a day and spending much of the other twelve hours figuring out new ways to act. Some of the praise put on these boys by her father had really been funny. "Making their way in the world." "Truly important young men, who mean something." "Men who you are not ashamed to say hello to on the street," etc.

When she went out with these fellows she tried hard to be agreeable and friendly. With a few of them it was not difficult. But there were those who made her boil. And when she boiled she came right out and told them what she thought. Once she had kicked one of them in the shins good and hard. That was something he would remember because it lasted for a few days. She wanted him to remember it.

There were those who made her tired. There were the dumb ones who amused her, and for whom she acted dumb so as to make them feel smart. It was all a slow endless belt with nothing really happening to get her excited until it suddenly stopped and Tommy was there.

This workday was ended now. Dorothy walked from the subway still thinking about him. When she got to the tenement the landlady was in the doorway and was saying, "Tired, dearie?"

"No, I feel swell."

"Oh, yes you do."

"Honest. Do you know why? All day long I've been thinking of Tommy. I could work all night, too. I'd just have to think of him and I'd forget all about how hard the work was."

"Maybe Tommy's been thinkin' of you today."

"He thinks of me every day."

"He's sent you something today, honey." The landlady's voice was thick. She gulped, and said, "I won't keep you waitin'. I slid it under your door."

Dorothy raced past her and up the steps. She snatched the letter and tore madly at the envelope.

"Dear
You mustn't work too hard now. It's hot and I know how those factories are. You take it easy, you hear me? Please listen to me. Maybe you can get a job at some country or seashore place where

you can be comfortable and you can also make good money. Go down to an employment agency and find out about it, because I don't like you to be working in that factory now ... "

She went through the next ten pages very swiftly, because they were all about her. She wanted to find out about him.

" ... so please take care of yourself. I'm taking a rest now. I got a very slight wound in my leg that doesn't amount to much and I'm behind the lines far enough back where the bombardment can't reach. The food is very good and the treatment we get is the best. Everybody is hopeful and any day now there may be a surprise. We're not doing half bad, although I wonder if the papers tell you that ...

"Of course you know what I'm thinking and how I feel while I write you this. We've already used up all the words between us. So by this time I can't do anything except think about it. And you know what I'm thinking...."

She put down the letter and shook her head slowly. You're a liar, Tommy, she kept saying, her lips forming the words but no sound coming. You're a liar, because you took a lot of time writing this letter and you tried too hard to make it sound as if nothing was wrong. You were lying to me, weren't you, Tommy?

I got a very slight wound in my leg.

You're lying, Tommy—lying.

Herb came up and found her sitting there on the bed staring stupidly at the floor. He could not get her to speak at first and even when she told him she could not express herself well.

"Come on, we'll go out for a ride. This does you a lot of good, doesn't it?"

"No, I want to stay here."

"I'll go then."

"No, I don't want you to go. I don't want to stay here all by myself."

"Will you cut it out?"

"Tommy's hurt, I know it. He's hurt."

"All right, that's what he said. He told you he was hurt. He wasn't lying. He—"

"No, I know differently. He's badly hurt. He's very—" She was getting all choked up and the tears were already there. He knew that if he didn't stop this now she was going to keep it up and it would get worse until it was so bad that he would be able to do nothing about it and every word he said, every gesture he made, no matter what, would make it worse. She would struggle and fight to hold back but finally she would reach a point where nothing would hold it back and all night long she would cry silently. It had happened once before. And in the morning she was a wreck and in the evening she was still sick.

So he knew that he had to stop this now. He pulled her to her feet and said, "Come on, we're going out."

"I don't want to go out."

"Come on."

"No."

"Well, if you think I'm going to stay here and—"

"Oh, go on then. You're terrible."

"Look, I'll take you down to see Wilda."

"Oh, who wants to see Wilda? From what you told me about her she'll probably start crying all over the place. That'll do me a lot of good." But anyway, Dorothy was coming out of it all right now and she was going downstairs with Herb. They were in the car and they were driving down to see Wilda.

It was only three days since Jean and Paul had gone away. Wilda was now alone in her apartment. They thought at first that she would have to be sent to a hospital, but she managed to brace and had gotten in touch with Herb. When he heard the news a queer feeling had come over him. He was not surprised. Not that he had figured on anything like this. But it did not seem too shocking. His only emotion was a slight pity for Paul, and a great pity for Wilda.

Now he was taking Dorothy down to see Wilda. It was the first time she was meeting any of his other acquaintances, outside of Paul. She said, "She better not start fighting with me."

"What's she fighting with you about? She doesn't even know you."

"I'm a woman, and so is Jean. A process of identification. Wilda probably hates every other woman in the world by this time."

But there was no fight, no scene. They found Wilda a white-faced, drooping, bewildered lady, whose eyes were tired, whose mouth was drawn down at the corners. She welcomed them with a weak smile, and when Herb introduced Dorothy, she kept this smile on her face.

Dorothy said, "Herb and I are old friends."

Wilda looked at her intently. And then at Herb. She said nothing,

Dorothy grinned. Herb said, "We're all in the same boat, Wilda. Dorothy's husband is fighting in Spain."

Wilda said, "Fighting—in Spain? Why?"

"He likes to fight," said Dorothy, shrugging.

Wilda stared at the floor, and then slowly got to her feet. "That's it," she said. "They all like to fight. They can't stand things being as they should be. We were happy, and he knew I loved him. He was all right when he was alone with me. He was good to me. Because he is good. He really is good. I'll always love him. Even if he never comes back to me—but that's why. Don't you see? That's why. It was too good. It was going along too nicely. When things are like that they break all at once."

She began to talk faster, and Herb tried to interrupt. She was going on, and what she said nearly came to be a babble of jumbled phrases. Dorothy motioned for Herb to do something about it, and he came over to put his hand on her shoulder and said, "You know what you need? You need some air. Let's go for a ride. It's nice out tonight."

"No," said Wilda, and she was still staring at the floor. "You and Dorothy go—please. Just let me stay hereby myself. That's all I want. I just want to stay here alone."

After they left, Wilda sat there staring at the light coming in and spreading itself on the carpet in a long, thin triangle. It faded, coming together and drowning in the dark green surface of the carpet. The room was without light. Wilda sat there seeing things as they had been years ago. Paul, eating, sleeping, talking, laughing. Paul touching her, kissing her, Paul going to work, Paul coming home at night, Paul sad, Paul happy. Paul in the night, Paul in the day, Paul in a gray suit, Paul in a brown suit. She sat there thinking of things that he had done, that he had said, that he had thought. And somehow, as, hours later, she wearily fell into bed, she could still see him, know what he was thinking and how he felt. Somehow she could not blame him. He was doing something he really did not want to do.

Nothing else entered her mind, no thoughts of Jean, or Herb, or this friend of Herb's, Dorothy, or anyone else, or anything else. Only this idea fixing itself there pounding away, so that as she was finally slipped through a succession of flat planes into a shallow level of sleep, she knew that in some way he was being forced, he really did not want to do this to her.

"I don't know why I took you to see her. It didn't do much good. There wasn't much sense to it."

"Maybe there was," said Dorothy. They were driving up to another apartment house. Herb was told that he would not be allowed to come back to his former rooms. The manager had said something about standards of behavior, the type of people he liked to have as tenants, etc. It was something not worth arguing about. Herb said that he would move out as soon as possible.

"How do you mean, maybe there was?"

"You might have suggested something, bringing me with you. As long as you could go and get yourself a girlfriend, she could go and get herself a boyfriend."

"She wouldn't do a thing like that."

"Maybe not, but it would do her a lot of good if she did. She's very good-looking. She's good-natured too, isn't she?"

"Wilda's all right," said Herb. He was thinking now that it was worse than he had figured at first. She looked terrible. She would make herself sick. It was a shame.

For a while they were very quiet. Then Herb said, "I've just been wondering where they could have gone."

Dorothy did not reply for a few moments. Then she said, "I'm sorry you took me to see Wilda. Now I feel terrible. I'll be thinking about her and—well, where do you think they went?"

"I have a feeling it's pretty far away."

"Are you worried?"

He was driving slowly. He said, "Yes. About Paul. I don't know why, but I'm sort of worried about Paul."

Dorothy went up with him to look over the new apartment. He made arrangements with the manager and in two days he would move in. As they left, Dorothy said, "You ought to be very comfortable there. Plenty of room. Too much for one person, I think."

"Yeah?"

"Yeah. Who do you think you are, a king or somebody, taking up all that space?"

"Well? Should I get a smaller place?"

"I didn't say that." She gave him a dirty look. "Besides, I think you're awfully selfish."

"So what do you want me to do?"

"Let me move in with you."

"All right."

"You really will?"

He turned and looked at her. She was grinning like a mischievous child and her eyes were snapping with countless dots of light.

"No," he said.

"Please?"

"No."

The car stopped in front of the tenement. She opened the door and jumped out and slammed it hard.

"Wait a minute," he said.

But she ran into the tenement and up the stairs. He started to get out of the car but held himself back. There was nothing he could say if he went up there. It was getting so now that he must begin slowly to break away from Dorothy.

She'd be living in my apartment, she'd be sleeping there too. I'd be sleeping there. How long does she think I can stand it, keeping myself back from her, why can't she see what she does to me? She must see it, no, she doesn't. She doesn't know. I better start this car and start driving before I lose my grip. She'll be all right tonight. At least she won't cry her eyes out and get all sick about Tommy. She'll stay up for a while thinking how no-good and selfish I am and then she'll be tired and go to sleep. And that's what she needs, sleep, Dorothy, sleep, dear.

In his room he pushed the bed close to the window. He raised the pillow so that he could lie there and look out and see the city lights. Down there they blazed and flickered green yellow blue orange red against the dark curtain of street and night sky.

While the lights flickered and blazed people were weeping, laughing, screaming and sighing, loving and hating. In a hundred years these people would be gone and the lights would be gone. But there would be new lights and there would be new people. The same story would go on. It had been going on for hundreds of thousands of years.

It was the story told of people in cities, on farms, in hills and in battlefields. They were good, they were bad, they were good again, and before they knew it they were dead and it didn't matter what they had been or what they had done. They might have gone through a lifetime without telling a lie, or they might have existed for twenty-three years and then gone on a killing spree and murdered five women and been electrocuted. But it didn't matter after the heart stopped beating. It was all over, this show, and someone else was just beginning it someplace else.

Everybody passed through it, kings and beggars, rats and elephants. When it was all over there was the body still, with the eyes open or the eyes closed. That didn't matter either. The eyes did not see anything. It was really all over and nothing could be done about it.

In a way it was unfair. The lights down there were lighting up streets and faces of people who were good and bad. But did it always work out that the good received good and the bad received bad? There had always been a lot of talk about this Heaven and Hell business. Well, the wise guys could laugh all they wanted to but it wasn't a bad idea. The chances were that it was just that, a lot of talk. But it wasn't a bad idea.

Soon he would push the pillow down and go to sleep. Then tomorrow he would wake up and go to work. The lights would be out down there, and one great big light would be working and letting all the dopes see what they were doing.

He stopped for a second and he pulled the brakes hard.

Who am I to call them dopes? Who do I think I am? Tomorrow I get up and eat breakfast like the rest of them after having washed my teeth and combed my hair like the rest of them. And I'll go out and walk with them on the street and read the same paper they read and find out the same things they find out. I'll go through the day working like they work and I'll feel the things they feel. I'll see some that I'll take one look at and hope they trip and break a leg. I'll see some that I hope find a job soon and maybe find a twenty-buck bill on the street. So the sun will shine down on all of us and we'll keep it up as long as we can and a lot of us will play over our heads while a lot of us roll up a string of errors and finally every last one of us will get taken out of the old ball game and then it won't make any difference.

It would make him feel good to shrug right now. That was just what he felt like doing—shrugging. So he shrugged and then pulled the pillow down and closed his eyes.

For three years he had been working side by side with this Helen Gillen and in that time all he knew of her was that she worked fairly hard and kept her mouth shut and did as she was told. Now he was sitting opposite her at lunchtime and they were sipping from glass straws dipped in long glasses of iced tea. And each minute that he spent with Helen Gillen strengthened his growing respect for her intelligence and steadiness of person, which qualities combined gave her a charm that Herb could only describe to himself as solid. She was that—solid.

"When Clark brought that idea up to you yesterday," she was saying, "did you see at once what he was trying to get across—that there is a distinction between being well-dressed and too well-dressed? Without any pictures at all he was trying to make that split—between a typical Broadway sharper and a stockbroker whose taste in clothes is influenced by English styles—did you get that right away?"

"Sure. I think the idea is pretty good—as far as that goes. It says 'Buy Shanville Shoes Because They Are Good-Looking But Not Too Good-Looking.' Then it elaborates on that idea and the typography scheme doesn't need any pictures except that photograph of their conservative-style shoe."

"Yes, but don't you agree that the appeal there is too negative? I'd say that a lot of your prospective buyers are going to feel put out because Shanville and Co. are calling them show-offs."

He stirred the straw idly. He thought it over. "You mean—considering the type of men who buy the magazine—"

"Yes, now just consider that—the type of men who buy the magazine."

He nodded. "I get it. Sort of a sock in the jaw to the ego."

"I don't think Mr. Edwinns will agree, though."

"Edwinns hasn't got it yet. I still have it in my desk. I think I'll work on it myself. I was going to send it down right after lunch. In fact, he would have had it by two o'clock sure if you hadn't brought up that point just now. Too bad for Clark. He burns up when that happens."

"Good."

"You don't like him?"

"I don't waste time not liking him. I detest him. From the minute I first saw him he's always given me the impression of a pig with a tin crown on its head, wallowing in mud."

"That's going pretty deep."

"Maybe you think that's why I criticized his idea just now."

"No, I don't."

She looked up from the straw. "Do you mean that?"

Herb nodded.

"Thanks. That really means a lot to me." Helen pushed the glass aside and leaned back in her chair. "It really does," she said.

He looked at her intently. His head nodded slightly.

Helen was wearing a creamy blue short-sleeved dress with a cream-colored belt and a pin to match the belt. He looked sideways at her as they walked slowly back to the office. She was doing all right.

After work he drove her home. She lived near Central Park and she asked him in. Her roommate was already fixing a cold supper and Helen introduced Herb to this rather short and fat but also somewhat handsome girl named Ethel Pine. Herb expected that Ethel talked a lot and she did start to talk as soon as she was introduced. She began slowly and then moved out to a racing stride in a tone that reminded Herb of knitting mills he had been in. There was a peculiar rhythm to this girl's speech, and it increased until she was really making time.

In between sentences Helen tried to get a word in but Ethel went right on. Among other things she insisted that Herb stay for supper and while he was considering this she went right on to the subject of what they had for supper and did Herb like this, did he like that, if he didn't like that she could always fix something that he liked because if she did say it herself she was a good cook and Helen would back her up on that, Helen better back her up on that or she'd put Dutch Cleanser in Helen's salad and besides she really was a good cook as they'd soon see when they sat down to supper and now it was getting near suppertime so she'd better go in the kitchen and come on, Helen, lend a hand there and you sit in here and listen to the radio, Herb, you can hear all the scores now, they come in over WABC.

She caught her breath and Herb sat down in a comfortable chair next to the radio. Helen and Ethel were in the kitchen. It was a spacious apartment for two people and the girls had it fixed up nicely. They had some interesting blue glassware and rugs that complimented the sofa and chairs, which were very dark purple.

They sat down at the table set up quickly in the center of the kitchen and almost right away they were talking and eating with enjoyment. Ethel jumped up from the table and ran in to change the station on the radio.

"She likes to hear swing music while she eats," said Helen. "She's crazy about swing music." She laughed.

They had a lot of fun. Herb began joking with Ethel and soon she was helpless, shaking continually while he cracked wise dryly. He was in good form tonight.

He pitched in and helped them wash and dry the dishes. They were parrying quips, and Helen was getting a big kick out of it. Herb and Ethel got along fine. Then afterwards Ethel called up a fellow and Helen whispered to Herb, "Wait'll you see this lad. He's an instructor in biology at NYU. Only twenty-six. But he's really something to look at." The way she said it sounded funny to him.

Ethel came in and said, "The light of my life has a lot papers to mark but he's gonna bring them over here. Do you drink, Herb?"

She opened a cabinet in the wall and he saw quite a few three- and four-dollar brands there. Ethel poured out some rock and rye.

After a while they were laughing a lot and the radio was too loud. Ethel was showing them how to do the "New York Hop," and Herb kept telling her to watch out or she'd fall. He kept telling her not to get excited, and to take it easy, she had a lot of time, and to watch her step. She finally did fall. Helen bent over double, holding her sides.

Finally this friend of Ethel's came in. He would have done all right in the movies. He was one of these guys with platinum-blond wavy hair and skin like a baby's. He was middle weight and not too tall. He came in with a briefcase and as soon as he entered he dropped the case and ran over to Ethel. He grabbed her and threw her down on the couch.

"It's been unbearable—this going on without you," he cried, his eyes wild. "I can't stand it, do you hear? I can't stand it."

"Terrible," said Helen. "Try again."

Ethel's friend got up off the couch and went to the door. He came in the same way again, and Ethel had no objections. Then he was introduced to Herb and his name was Norman something. He said that he hated to be so low about all this but there were two things he had to do this evening. He had to mark the papers, he said, and then he looked at Ethel. Herb said that maybe he could help Norm mark the papers. Finally after a big argument over the best method they sat around the table and Norm read out the right answers while Herb, Ethel and Helen made checks and crosses on the papers.

After they finished with the papers they sat around and argued on things in general. This Norm turned out to be a brilliant guy with three degrees and no fancy lace. They argued about industry, politics, labor, love, general human behavior, and finally they played bridge.

Norm made some dumb plays and had a few fights with Ethel. Then Helen stood up and said, "I feel like drinking some more."

"Not rock and rye. A lot of syrup in your stomach. You'll feel like a sick fish, I'm telling you." Herb followed her to the liquor cabinet. She turned her head slightly to him.

"It's getting late. We'll go in the other room."

"Not polite."

She turned around and looked over his shoulder at Ethel, who was giving her a signal to take Herb and go in the other room. She laughed.

"Come on," she said.

He followed her into the bedroom. There were two beds with green quilts, there was light green wallpaper and two original sketches which he admired. She said that Ethel had bought them during a sidewalk exhibit in the Village. Herb stood there admiring the sketches and then Helen was behind him and smoothing his hair.

"I wonder how those artists eat," he said.

"Are you really worried about it?"

"Sometimes I am," said Herb. "You are, too. I bet you find yourself at times worrying about people who don't have enough to eat."

"No, I'm mean that way. But I do reserve a certain amount of my income, my enormous income, for charity each year, don't you?"

"No special amount. When they ask me, I usually give, but I don't give enough. I should give more. Of course, if I really want to look at it the right way, I should give a lot more."

"Get undressed and then we'll talk."

They got undressed. He came in from the bathroom in his shorts and stretched his arms, yawning. Helen pushed her arms through silk and said, "You very tired?"

Herb nodded. He slowly crawled onto the bed and grinned at her as she came over to him. She put herself down upon him and kissed his lips. Then she rolled over and they rested side by side, looking up at the ceiling.

"You're not in love with me, are you, Herb?"

"No."

"I'm glad. It's really better."

"How about you?" He wriggled comfortably into the pillow.

"No." She bounced her spread fingers against one another and said, "No, I care for someone I can never have."

"Tell me about it."

"No."

"You don't like to talk about it?"

"I would like to talk about it," she said. "I'd like to tell it to everyone who wants to listen. But afterwards, I'd be sorry. I'd tell myself that I shouldn't have said anything at all. No, I don't want to talk about it."

"Then listen to me."

"Go on."

"I—no, I don't want to talk about it either. Right now I want to forget about it. I'm in the same boat as you."

They were quiet.

He said, "When I'm with you I want to forget about it."

"That's right. I feel that way too."

"Then it's all right," he half-questioned, half-told her. "Of course it's all right."

They were quiet. She moved nearer him. In a little while there was a knock on the door and Ethel yelled, "We're coming in to get the mattress."

She came in with Norm and they pulled the mattress off the other bed and took it into the living room. Before Norm closed the door Helen said, "Now if there's anything else you need take it now and don't come disturbing us every five minutes."

"Good night, dear," said Norm. "Good night, Herb." He closed the door.

Helen reached up and turned out the lamplight. The room was dull dark. Only a thin blade of breeze entered to cut through the thick city heat. The dull throbbing of the streets, the pavements, the countless assortments of brick and steel and wood, the throbbing sound made by the actual stillness of all this, came steadily, accompanied by another throbbing that was the combined force of pulse beat and breathing, millions of people living and in motion.

Alone, Dorothy was unable to sleep. She got up and drank a glass of water. She drank another glass of water. Puzzled as to why she was so thirsty, she forced a third glass down.

Now go and take a fourth, you sap, and you'll be going all night. So thirsty, so tired, but can't sleep, can't drink any more. Want someone here with me, want Tommy, want Tommy so very much, can't sleep, can't do anything without Tommy. You're hurt bad, aren't you? Aren't you? Say, Dorothy, I was lying to you, I am really hurt bad and very bad. Out of so many bullets and so many men you had to get hit, didn't you? I'm sore at you now. I'm not speaking to you for being so clumsy and for lying to me. I'm sore at you and I'm sore at Herb. Bad Tommy bad Herb. Awfully bad, mean, thoughtless, spiteful, disgusting Herb because you won't come up here and take care of me while Tommy is away. Even when you must know that right after Tommy comes you, and I do want you awfully bad right now because but go on and keep your old apartment for yourself and I hope you go away in the morning and leave the bathtub running and the whole place gets filled with water. Oh, Tommy Tommy Tommy it's like a headache and a stomachache and a cramp in my leg and a toothache too, everything hurts all at once and it's all your fault. Just you wait till I get my hands on you for doing this to me, you you, oh, Tommy, Tommy, please come back. Run away, desert, please. No, Dorothy, you rat, snake, skunk, don't tell him to do that. He must never do anything like that. But I do want him to, yes, I do want you to, Tommy, run away, sneak away from them and get on a boat and come back to me. It's wrong, Tommy, it's wrong if you do it, but I want you to do it, please run, come running back to me.

Tears formed a broken stream on her cheeks as she fell asleep.

CHAPTER XIV

When the eyes are closed it hurts worse, because then it can't be seen, and there is only the physical pain. This mounts higher until the nails dig hard into the palms, the teeth come together trying to press one another back into the gums. Sweat bursts from the head, around the mouth in welling beads that break and form a glassy pool on the stretched and trembling flesh.

But when the eyes are opened the physical pain is lessened because then the bed slopes down suddenly and there is a plateau where there should be a hill. Why should there not be these two long white hills on the bed? There was only one now. Where the other should have been there was only this white plateau. This wonder takes the mind off the pain.

In the bed to the right there was a boy who had been hit by shrapnel. He would die. All day long he kept on moaning and reciting poetry. Some of it was very good, and from the way this boy recited it, Tommy imagined that it was original. At times it was so very good and true that it took his mind off the pain and the leg cut away from his body. The boy was an American, but Tommy didn't know his name. He wanted to ask the nurse but every time she came around his thigh was burning and blasted, punctured deeply by countless needles and tiny hammers, and he could only ask her if she would do something for him.

This was on the third day after the operation. Yesterday he had written to her. For two hours his mind had cleared and he had been able to scribble in his jerky, fast handwriting, forgetting the pain, the effort, the strain, and he had written that letter. Afterwards his arm had ached, the leg hurt mercilessly, and he was very sick, his fever had mounted.

From the bed to his right there came a faint voice that grew louder until it was clear and resonant, even though it contained the twang of aching effort on weakening lungs in a weakening body. Tommy listened carefully. It was something about men walking on grass and men walking on asphalt, men marching through grass and men marching through streets, houses crumbling, babies crying, mothers dying, blood on all the streets and pus seeping through the grass. The seasons will roll too slowly again, again there will be winter, with the snow on the battlefields and the ice forming on fingers and stiff gloves, with clear ice and white ice forming on the rusty sides of tired cannon and battered tanks. But winter will pass and spring will pass, another winter and another spring will pass, many winters and many springs will glide by, and from this earth new roots will spring, new hopes will rise, new dreams to float themselves across the skies, above this earth from which new tree, new flesh, with slow, unceasing gentle push will rise...

"Hey—"

"... the wind again will creep and faster—"

"Hey—"

"... and faster—"

"Hey, listen, I'm calling you."

"Me?"

"Yeah. I can't get up. Have to lie here on—my back. Do you feel like talking?"

"Yes. I ought to know you. You're American, aren't you? What's your name?"

"Tom Nicola. I was with the Garibaldi Legion. I got transferred a few times and I was with—"

"Can you see me?"

"No, I can't move my head that far over."

"I can't see you either. My name is Alfred Hampson. I was with the George Washington Brigade."

"How long have you been here?"

"I don't know. I'll never get out, though. I can't last more than another day." His voice was much lower when he spoke than when he recited poetry. "I'm all smashed up." When he said that he gurgled slightly. Then, his voice very low, he said, "It's been a year now since I came over. I didn't expect to last this long, after the first attack. It's pretty bad, isn't it?"

"Yeah—their planes, their—"

"What's wrong with you, Tom?"

"My leg—off."

A nurse came over and told Tom not to talk to him. It was a strain. Tom nodded. The other boy kept on talking but Tom did not answer. The voice faded.

"Why don't you answer me? I'm asking you again how old you are and what you did before you came over. Why don't you answer me? Tell me why you came and what you are going to do when they send you back. Sure, they'll send you back now. Maybe you can do something for me. I have some things I've written that I'd like you to take back and give to my people. They live in Boston. I was doing graduate work at Harvard when I decided to come. I was trying for my Master's degree in English literature. If I could go back now, if I could go back—but I don't want to. Do you want to? Do you? Why are you quiet like that? Don't you want to talk with me? Come on, let's be pals and talk to each other. I don't have much more time and I feel like talking and listening. It's better than just lying here and—besides, you don't want me to start in again with that crapped-up poetry, do you? Do you? I wish you'd say something, I'd like—"

He started to gurgle. It lasted for too long a time, and Tom wondered if he should call the nurse. But then she was coming over. He saw her moving fast past his bed and then was beyond the range of his eye, although he could hear her moving around the next bed. Then another nurse was coming. In a few minutes the soft sound of the rubber-tired trolley came from the doorway to the left, and then it was passing Tom's bed. He could hear them talking softly, and then the rustle of sheets, the lifting movement as the body was placed on the trolley.

Tom waited as they adjusted the bed. The trolley was moving out toward the center of the room, turning left, and there it was, passing his bed, the trolley, with the body on it, moving quietly down toward the door.

In a little while the nurse came over and said, "You can take some broth now, can't you?"

"No. I really can't. I know I couldn't hold it."

"Try."

He did not argue. She had been very kind, they had all been very kind, they tried their best, they suffered along with you, it seemed. Besides, he was too weak to argue.

The broth came and he took it down and brought it up.

"Oh, that's too bad," said the nurse. She took the towel from beneath his chin. She wiped his mouth while he grinned weakly with loosely closed lips.

"I told you," he murmured.

"We'll try again later," said the nurse as she took the tray away.

The pain started in again and kept on going deeper and deeper, then higher, as if it was trying to reach up and grab his heart. It moved about in a circle, and he moved with it. The pain and he were moving about in a circle. They were racing each other. Maybe he could get ahead of it, move out and in front of it in that circle. Now he was going ahead. He remembered one time when he had read in the sports pages about this running duel between Cunningham and Venzke. They had been going at it for some time and this was an important race.

That's right, Tom, he said to himself, think about Cunningham and Venzke and not about the leg.

This was an important race and Gene said he was out to win this time and well of course he was out to win. If he wasn't out to win what was the use of starting the race at all. That was a dumb thing to say. Or had he said it? Well, he had said something like that. Anyway, Tom had read the sports pages and had become interested and had bought a ticket.

They were running. It was a sight, the bodies moving steadily around that oval, the steady drone of the crowd; their bodies moving, their legs—

Their legs.

Anyway, they were going around in that circle, like himself and the pain. Cunningham moved out in front. Then Venzke. Then Venzke moved out more. A space between them widening. A space between himself and his pain widening. He was going to move out in front of his pain in this circle in which they were running just like Gene Venzke had moved out in front of Cunningham in that race that night. But finally Cunningham had won, the picture coming to Tom now of Glenn Cunningham chugging down there, coming up on Venzke as the tape stretched out and beating him by not more than a yard.

The pain was coming up on him now, he would have to go a little faster. He was still out in front. He could still reverse it. He could be Cunningham and the pain could be Venzke. He kept switching it around. He went over that race again. It had been a good race. Gene had said that he was out to win, and he had run that way, as if he really wanted to win.

Well, Tom would run that way also. He wanted to win. He would beat the pain out. If he really wanted to win he would beat the pain to the tape. Gene had said that he wanted to win. Gene had lost the race.

Gene did lose that race oh it's got me bad now it's high, why does it have to reach up there and keep on going up like that, up, up, into me. It should hurt only where it's cut. That's fair. It shouldn't keep on moving up into me like this. It's ahead of me now in the circle it's ahead of me.

This was the way he came to realize that he was being forced back, and he understood, lying there, that after all this pain was reaching up into his heart. He could feel it now, coming up, boring, reaching up into him, and he held his breath and he could feel it coming up and taking him.

So this is the way it gets you. You can take so much and no more. Sooner or later you discover that you've had too much and too much blood has been let out of your body, too much life with the blood.

He lapsed into a hazy hanging state, and when the nurse came she saw that he was very pale, he scarcely recognized her. One of the doctors passed by and she asked him to look at Tommy. He looked at Tommy and then he turned to the nurse and shrugged.

A little while later Tommy came out of it for a few minutes. He started to talk. A nurse came over. He did not look at her. He was talking fast and gurgling.

"... Dorothy—"

Then there was no more talking. There was nothing. He held on for a moment, and then he relaxed, with no more pain. His head moved slightly, and the arm tried to move up, but fell back upon the bed, the wrist dangling over the side.

They brought in the flat trolley to take the body away.

CHAPTER XV

Slowly Wilda was coming around. Herb took her out a few times, and he veered her away from the subject that was tearing at her. They went to the movies and afterwards Herb did most of the talking. Wilda listened and sometimes answered. But she was a different woman. She seemed to be thinking a lot. At least, mused Herb, after leaving her, she had not collapsed in total surrender. Something was holding her up.

There was a half chance that Wilda would come out of it completely. She was showing a lot of fight. He never expected this, because Wilda had always impressed him as being the type who blows up like a bag of wind and then bursts completely. She was surprising him now.

They were coming back from a movie and she had just said that she didn't care for any ice cream. Then she was talking slowly, but with a careful pace and a steadiness of voice so that he knew that she had been thinking this out, perhaps for days.

"Any day now I'll get a letter or a telegram. You'll see, Herb. I don't think you will, but I will. He won't be able to hold in any longer. He'll have to tell me. And when he does, it will be the truth. He's always been good to me and he'll be good to her. But he'll be honest too. That's what he is, honest."

"Do you call this honest, what he's done?"

"That's the only thing that's puzzling me."

"What do you mean, puzzling you?"

"If he had known this wasn't right, he never would have done it." She raised her voice a little. "I think that's why he did it. In some way it was for him the only thing to do."

Herb wanted to tell her that she was talking like a fool. But it would do her a lot of good to think this way. As long as she kept thinking that Paul was all right, that what he had done was not as bad as it looked, then she'd be all right. Of course she was merely rationalizing, and her thoughts of what was going to happen were nothing more than wishful thinking. He took her hand and pressed it, smiling at her like a brother. She looked back at him and there was nothing for her to say.

Up in her room she looked at his picture. He was leaning against the side of a big tri-motored monoplane. He was wearing a transport pilot's dark blue uniform and cap. At that time he had a mustache and he was grinning. Behind the plane a part of the hangar was visible. For the background to Paul there was this plane and the hangar. She could also see the figures of a few pilots.

Wilda brought the picture closer to her face. She talked to Paul. She asked him what was wrong. She asked him what Jean had done to him. He leaned against the plane grinning at her, but she did not see the grin. She saw pain in his face.

When he left Wilda that night, Herb decided to get a good nine hours sleep. He drove up to his apartment, but then kept on going, turned around twice and continued up to Harlem. He had not seen Dorothy for three days.

The landlady told him that Dorothy had gone out and would not be back till late. He told her to just say that Herb had called. Going home he felt peculiarly relieved. On the following night he had a date with Helen Gillen. She slept over at his apartment. The night after that he drove halfway up to Dorothy's address and then turned around and spent the evening with a few friends at a bar. He had a lot to drink and he was hearing too many echoes as he left. But he got to his room all right and the next morning he did not feel heavy.

But in the evening there was this urge to go up there and see her. There was also a burden of guilt gaining weight as he debated with himself. At last he got in his car and rode up there.

The landlady met him at the door. "You can't see her now. She's sick. That poor kid came home from work today more dead than alive. I called a doct—hey, you can't go up to—now you come back—"

He opened the door softly and the first thing he saw was the paleness of her face, the dark blueness beneath her closed eyes. The landlady was coming up the steps.

"I told you—" the landlady was saying.

"It's all right," said Herb. "I can stay here. You go out."

"But I—"

"Look, you go out."

She went out. Herb put his hand to Dorothy's forehead. She was warm. She opened her eyes and said, "Hello, ugly."

"What's the matter?"

"Take a look. Can't you see what's the matter? And thanks for coming around. Next time wait till Christmas."

"Is it your stomach?"

"I don't think so. I'm very hungry now."

"Do you want something to eat?"

"When I'm hungry I usually want something to eat."

"I'm afraid to get you anything. We'll wait and hear what the doctor says."

"Oh, the doctor. I forgot. I've got to put up with that too, don't I?"

"Yes."

"Why?"

"Because the doctor will make you well again."

"You think so?"

"Yes, Dorothy."

Don't look at me like that, Dorothy. It hurts bad enough. You had a good time, last night, didn't you, Herb. You got drunk with the boys. And the night before that you had a lovely time with Helen. You've been enjoying yourself, haven't you, Herb. Please don't look at me like that, Dorothy.

"Yes, Dorothy," she mimicked him.

"What happened to you?" he said.

"I felt it coming on at lunchtime. I had a headache and I was dizzy. When I came home I was sick, that's all."

There were footsteps on the stairs. A doctor was coming in. A tall man, he brushed long hair out of his eyes and moved over to the bed.

"Now let's see what's wrong with this beautiful young lady," he said. "First let's see your tongue."

She put out her tongue but the doctor had turned quickly and shouted at Herb, "Who are you?"

He was startled, and before he could answer, Dorothy, nearly giggling, said, "He's my husband."

"Oh."

"Is that okay with you, Doc, me being her husband?"

The doctor ignored him. He was giving Dorothy a careful examination. Herb did not know that he was frowning worriedly at Dorothy until she caught him looking at her. She made a face at him.

The doctor stood up.

He waited for Herb to say, "Well, Doc?"

"You work hard, don't you?" the doctor said to Dorothy, and he gave Herb a dirty look.

"Awfully hard, Doctor. I've asked my husband to get a job but he just sits around all day and goes to the poolroom—"

The doctor turned a long, accusing nose in Herb's direction. His eyebrows were raised as he noticed the Palm Beach suit and tan and white buckskin shoes.

"Hit the numbers recently, didn't you?"

"That's all he does, Doctor," said Dorothy, "and I don't get a cent of it. He plays the numbers and when he wins on that he plays the horses. He's no good."

"I'll say he's no good. Young man, have you any money left from that lucky number?"

Herb figured that he might as well nod.

The doctor said, "You're going to go out and spend it on food and some clothes for this poor girl. Then you're going out to look for a job. I'm not charging you for this visit, but if this girl is working by next week and you're still loafing around, I'm going to hunt you up and punch you in the nose."

"Yes, Doctor," said Herb.

As the doctor turned to leave, Herb slipped a ten-dollar bill into his coat pocket. The doctor smiled at Dorothy, "You're all right, girlie. You just take a good rest and throw this bum out on his ear if he doesn't get busy and work for you." He glared at Herb. "Remember what I said." He left.

Dorothy looked at Herb with a poker face. "You heard what he said."

"Yeah, I heard what he said and I'm gonna do like he said. You're quitting that swell job you got."

"Now isn't that lovely." She folded her arms and sank deeper in the pillow.

"You heard me, Dorothy, you're quitting the job. You're going to quit this room too. No arguments, please."

She won't like this, she'll get angry because she'll say it's charity and so she'll—

"Where do we go from here?" said Dorothy. "First, I wish you'd get me something to eat. I'm really awfully hungry."

Herb was making a hundred and a quarter a week. He had never made more than that, and he had lived up to nearly every penny of it. Jean had been of no little help in disposing of the money, and now that she was gone, Herb found that he had a little extra cash on hand. When he took Dorothy down to his apartment, he was wondering if he could afford to keep her there and go find another room for himself. There was the possibility of a legal entanglement from this business of Jean and Paul and he might have to lay down a few bucks there. But one thing was sure. He was not going to stay in the apartment with Dorothy.

He opened the door and let her in. She walked to the center of the room and looked around. "Not bad," she said.

"Don't stand around. Get in bed. You're sick, you know."

"Oh, am I? Gee."

"Please get in bed, Dorothy."

"Oh, wait a minute, will you? Let me look the place over. I don't know if I'm satisfied with it yet. I'm sort of particular about these things, you know."

"Come on, come on."

"I'm going to take a shower first. I'm filthy."

"You're going to get right in bed and no buts. Let's go."

She pushed him away. "I said I was going to take a shower."

He shook his head. "No you're not."

"Oh, no?"

He grinned at her and then before she knew what he was going to do he had picked her up easily in his arms. She turned an insolent face to him and said, "I suppose you think you're strong, don't you?"

Herb carried her into the bedroom and turned on the bed light. "I'm going out and I'll bring you back one of those hot suppers all ready to eat. Here's some magazines." He threw them on the bed. "What else do you want?"

"Lemonade."

"You'll get lemonade. What else?"

"Toys." She put a finger to her mouth and wagged her head. "A doll, a teddy bear—"

When Herb came back he carried a large paper bag. He took the food into the kitchen and reheated it. When he came into the bedroom he carelessly threw on the bed a large shaggy doll with a blonde head and a funny face. Dorothy put down the magazine and started to talk to the doll.

She heard Herb moving about in the kitchen and all of a sudden there was a crash and swearing followed by a dismal silence followed by the sound of hands picking up the pieces of three broken dishes.

"You must have dropped something," Dorothy shouted.

"A real comedienne, aren't you?"

He brought in her dinner on a tray. She had chicken broth and then lamb chops, baked potato, peas, and toast and tea, with cookies.

"You'll get your lemonade later."

She did not start to eat right away. She looked from the tray to his face, then to the tray, then to his face again.

"Eat," he said.

"I can't manage this tray and eat my soup at the same time. I'll spill it all over myself. You'll see."

"Now wait a minute. Let's look the situation over. All right, you hold the tray steady and I'll feed you the soup."

He started to feed her the soup and she got a laughing spell with a mouthful of soup and had to swallow it quickly. He tried to keep a straight face but at last he broke out in a grin. Then scowling, he said, "Next time you'll choke."

While she tore at the lamb chop, he sat on the side of the bed and read the paper. He went into the other room and turned on the radio. He came back and resumed his reading. Dorothy sipped tea and took part of the paper.

After a while she said, "I feel a lot better."

Herb put down the paper. "You do?"

"Mmm hmmm. Do I look it?"

He nodded. Color was coming back into her cheeks. Her eyes were not so bright and wide now. She got out of bed.

"Hey, where you going?" He put out a hand to stop her.

"Take it easy, greasy," she said, getting away from him and going into the bathroom. "I have an important appointment," she said and closed the door with a slam.

Herb went up to the bathroom door and shouted, "Did you go in there to take a shower?"

"No, I didn't go in here to take a shower."

"All right then."

"Are you happy? As long as you're happy, you know."

He went back into the bedroom and started to read the papers again.

Later they were listening to a program of good music followed by a news broadcast. And then it was half-past eleven.

"Are you sleepy, Dorothy?"

"No, dear." She took his hands and pulled him toward her. He would not come any closer and she said, "Kiss me."

"No."

"Oh, please kiss me, Herb. Honest, you're so mean." She pulled him to her again, and he grinned and kissed her lightly, but she held him against her and ran her hand through his hair, then pulled him even closer, keeping his lips against hers. He broke away, trying not to look like a bewildered, frightened boy. He was breathing hard.

"You're sleeping with me tonight," she said, holding his wrists.

"That's what you think." He got up and took a few steps toward the other room. Then before he realized it, he had whirled, gone back to the bed, put his arms gently about her, and was kissing her again. In the next instant he had regained control of himself, but she was holding him down against her.

"Dorothy, I can't—I—"

"Oh, you can't. Oh, I see." She tried to grin lewdly, but it was impossible for her to grin lewdly. "That means you're unable, is that it?"

"All right then, I'm unable."

She stopped grinning. "Stop being stupid. You can't sleep on that sofa in there. You'll be all broken up in the morning."

"Don't worry about it."

He went into the living room.

Soon in the apartment the lights were out and there was a

hesitant silence, as if it was expanding slowly, waiting to explode. They were both awake, and she was waiting for him to come into the bedroom. He tried to fall asleep there on the sofa but he kept thinking of her in there and himself in here, and why he must stay here and not go into the room where Dorothy slept.

Slowly the silence ceased to expand. It died down to a thin quiet broken only by an auto passing on the street below, a passing tread of feet in the hall, the rattle of the subway, and then as gray moved up into the sky, the restless groaning of a city waking up.

CHAPTER XVI

On a green Pacific streaked with blue flashes, banded with lines of white gold twisting like maddened snakes, a white ship moved steadily toward the west. It was going toward the East, to China.

At the rail Paul Schuen looked down at the water and wondered how deep it was. They said that at some points this Pacific job was four miles deep. It must take a long time to get down to the bottom of a pool like this. What was all the water for? Suppose someday it got itself together and made a rush back on the land. That was a nice thing to suppose. He watched the water twist away from the side of the boat and then come back, drawn by the rush of the propeller.

In a few minutes Jean would come up from the cabin and walk along the deck until she found him. They would stand here at the rail together looking out at the water. They wouldn't say much. But any minute now, he expected it. He could see it as clearly as he could see the clear water when it jumped up against the white portside. He could hear her coming up and starting slowly, then faster, her voice rising in this rebellion that was gathering itself within her.

But things happened this way. When you run away, you run away. You don't care where you are going. After your course is charted, after you're on your way, then you begin to think things over and you wonder where you are going and why you are going there. That was Jean's situation. His was different.

He was going to China. He was going to meet some of the boys there and then the Chinese Government would pay him good money to fly a plane and fight the Japanese aviators.

Sooner or later he would have to tell Jean this. Right now all she knew was that they were running away. But he must tell her and he might as well get it off his chest right now, because she was walking down the deck and coming toward him.

It might be easier than he had expected, after all. She was smiling at him and she looked very well, as if she was enjoying this immensely. From a small tan beret her blonde hair moved out in a smart wave onto her cheeks, which were slightly tan and gently rouged. There was not the usual excess of lipstick today, and she had very little mascara. The sea wind slanted her a little and she grabbed at the rail for support. He laughed.

"Don't let it throw you."

She put her hand on his on the rail. "It's a lot of fun, isn't it?"

"Wait'll we hit one of those storms. You'll see your fun."

"Oh, no."

"Oh, yes. Wait'll we run into the storm area, and—"

"Paul, you're mean." She turned away from him, and looked disagreeable for the instant.

"Oh, I'm just kidding. There's really nothing to worry about. We'll be there in about four days, and—"

"Paul—"

"Mmm?"

"Paul, we made a big mistake taking this trip. I did—"

"The baby?"

She nodded.

"Don't worry about that," he said. "Four days more and it's all over. And you've been doing fine, so far."

"Where do we go from there?"

Here it was. He tried to look away from her as he said it, but she was pulling him around and he was saying, staring at her, "Well, I figured we'd stay there. We need money, you know. I couldn't make very definite financial arrangements, because we were in such a hurry, and—you know how things were. So I contacted an aviation outfit in China, and I'll do some work there. We can—"

"In China?"

"Why not?"

"But the war—" Her voice dipped slowly, then rose with a tremble.

"China's a big place. We won't be anywhere near the battle areas. We'll be comfortable and you won't be lonesome. I have friends there and you'll meet their wives. It'll be all right."

"But how long do we have to stay?" Her voice was still rising and the tremble was increasing.

"Why?"

"Why?" She almost shouted that. He could see that Jean was

getting excited. "Do you think I want to stay there forever. We—I—want to get back. And the baby—he'll grow up like a Chink. Say, I don't want to stay there, Paul. I thought we were just taking a trip. Say, do you think I'm going to settle down and live there? I'm not doing that. Are you—"

"No, I'm not intending to live there, dear. But I've got to find a secure position. My New York job is shot now. I ran out on them right in the midst of a rush period, and, they'll never take me back. This is the only other opening I have. And it's good. I'll be making some real money now."

"But we won't stay there long, will we? Promise me, we—"

"Jean, I can't make any promises, because I'm looking out for us from the practical side. It'll be all right. You'll see."

"I hope so." She was looking at the horizon and trying to figure it out. She had so many questions to ask him about this that she did not know how to start. She had started the wheel going, but he had increased the speed, and now they were spinning around and she was going so fast that she could only cling mutely for support and wait with frightened eyes for what would happen next.

For a few minutes more Jean stood there at the rail with Paul. Then she said that it was better for her to be in the cabin. Besides, the sea was getting rough. Wasn't it? He nodded, took out a pipe, began to fill it. She waited for him to say something. He bit into the black stem and murmured that perhaps it was better for her to be in the cabin as much as possible. He wanted to stay here for just a little while longer. He'd be in soon. She left him and went back to the cabin.

The tobacco smoke and the salt air felt clean and strong in his mouth and throat. He looked out at the rising water and then up at the clouds. Already he was in a plane and it was a dependable machine, strong, new, the motor smooth, the guns—the guns—

Just like a kid, he thought, I'm out for a thrill.

But it was not a thrill he sought now. He too was in this wheel racing around with Jean. And the wheel was going around too fast. He did not know what he sought now. The wheel was moving too fast for him.

CHAPTER XVII

All days could not possibly be like this. To get up late, to make breakfast slowly, to eat it slowly, to loll around all day and read and listen to the radio, to go out with him in the evening and then go to sleep at night and wake up in the morning knowing that there were no eight hours of labor ahead to tear away at the arms, the eyes, the brain.

Yet here it was. She was living in Herb's apartment and every day was a twenty-four-hour blessing. He came home in the evening with a paper and she waited for his steps in the hall. When he opened the door she ran to him, threw her arms about his neck, and kissed him lovingly.

He would return those kisses, he would drop the paper and there would be the sudden tightening of his arms about her, and then that instant when his face would tighten, he would look at her and let his arms fall away.

"Why do you do that?"

He would shake his head slightly, say something quickly to change the subject, and they would soon be having an argument. And then they would be going out to a restaurant, and after that to a movie, or on some nights to an open-air concert, or sometimes just for a ride. She would ask him to stop the car. He would refuse. She would ask him if he felt healthy tonight. He would say no. He felt weak, tired, low. Dorothy could fix that up, she would say. So could a good night's sleep, he would say, and kiss her and ask her would she please be good?

They went on this way for two weeks. Then one day Herb came back to find no Dorothy running to kiss him, no Dorothy in the apartment, only a little note.

"Dear no-good bum:
Guess what I went and done. I packed up all my things and went home, because I don't like your old dirty apartment and my place is nicer than yours anyway. So there. If you want to come up here

and fight about it I'll be receiving tonight from seven until nine. No cards.

Dorothy.

He put the note in his pocket and went out to eat. But he wasn't hungry. He had been hungry when he had left the office, and now he had no appetite. He went down to his car and got in. What he wanted to do was press the accelerator down to the floor and turn the wheel all the way around, not caring where he went or what he hit. But he drove up there and went in.

"Listen, I have a right to do what I want. I felt like leaving."

"Just like that you felt like leaving."

"Yes, and you can't do a thing about it."

"All right, I won't. I suppose you'll go back tomorrow and start work again."

"That's right."

"Then in another week you'll be in bed again and I'll have to come up here and take you back to the apartment."

She did not answer that. She looked away from him and now it was gripped hard, it was hurting, there was no laughter to break in upon this and cover it up. It lasted too long, and they both wanted to stop it but they could not.

"If you need me you know where to call me," Herb said.

She managed to keep her eyes turned away from him as he left, and then it was nothing but sitting there and thinking about him, then about Tommy, and more about Tommy, and when would she get the next letter from Tommy, and how tired she was, and how slowly the hours were going to pass from now on.

Herb went to this favorite bar of his and he began to drink. A few acquaintances came up and tried to make conversation but he discouraged them. He was enjoying it now, taking it not too fast, and it was feeling good down there, and not rising on him too much. He was on his eighth when he noticed that from the side someone was looking at him intently. He turned and thought he recognized the guy, who was young and a little taller than himself, very broad.

"Remember me?" said the guy.

"Yeah, I think I do." He couldn't exactly place this one, but he connected him up with something interesting.

"I'm George Green."

"Oh. Green? Yeah—" But he still couldn't place him.

"You remember," said George. "We had a little fun together one night up in your apartment. Your wife—"

"Oh yeah, yeah. How ya doin'? Have a drink."

"Thanks." George ordered a brandy and soda. He said, "How did that business turn out?"

"She went away with him. I don't know where they are."

"How about his wife? It's a pity about her."

"Yeah." Herb threw liquor down his throat. "Yeah, it's a pity all right."

George refused to let Herb buy him another drink. He had a little money, he said, and he had come into this bar for the purpose of drinking and paying for his own drinks. He sounded very straight and as they stood there, George began to talk in a steady, slow stream of words that sounded clean.

"I guess as far as you're concerned, anything I say about Jean is all right," he said. Herb nodded, and George went on, "Well, I feel this way. If she wanted me now, I don't care where she is, but I'd go to her. You don't believe that, do you? You don't look as if you believe it."

"I believe it. I'm looking this way because it wasn't so long ago that I felt the same way."

"What's she got, anyway?"

"I used to ask myself that question over and over again. It doesn't bother me now. They said you had quite a time of it with my friend Paul."

"Yeah, I ran into real trouble there. He nearly killed me. I had to go to a doctor." He opened his mouth and pointed to where the teeth were gone. Then he shrugged. "I don't mind. You know, that guy seemed all right. From the way he talked and the way he fought, he seemed to be a pretty fair guy."

"He's all right."

"So he went away with her."

"That's what he did, all right." He had the glass half raised, but he put it down and said, "Maybe you know something about it. Did you hear anything while you were there? Do you know anything?

Myself, I don't care, but his wife, this Wilda, she's completely in the dark. You know, she never expected anything like this. It came all of a sudden."

"All I know is that after I went down I was just lying there half out but I do remember one thing that went on. She said something about going away, and he said no, but then he stopped and hesitated and then said that was the only thing they could do."

"That's what he said?"

"Well, not the exact words, but that's what he meant. So I don't think it was planned, not by him, anyway."

"Not by him? What do you mean?"

"Jean must know what she's doing. She's smart." He tilted his glass.

"She thinks she's smart," said Herb. The twelfth drink went down like melted butter.

Talk switched to other things and Herb did most of the listening. But while he was listening he was thinking about Jean and Paul, and he was reaching conclusions and wishing he could face them and substantiate these conclusions.

George Green had the blues now. He poured out his troubles and poured in more brandy. It seemed that everything was against him now, still no job, no prospects, no money, no nothing. No friends, nothing.

"I wake up late in the morning and by that time it's eleven. I go to sleep again. When I get dressed, when I finally do get on the street, it's about two. And I'm still tired. I get to see about two or three people and it's five. This is every day, mind you. Every day in the week." He did not have the money to open up an office, and if he did open up an office, the money would go like water and he would be deeper in debt. There was nothing open to him.

"Let's go," said Herb. He paid their bill and George said, "I can't let you do that," but did not move a hand near his pocket, and did not say thanks.

He walked alongside Herb and finally Herb said, "Where do you stay?"

"Oh, I got a room." George's eyelids dropped, but he was walking straight, not without obvious effort, however. "I jus' about manage."

He tagged along and. Herb said, "Tell you what. You can stay at my place and that'll save you a little. I got room. You can come over tonight and then tomorrow you can bring your belongings over."

"Tha'll be swell. Tha'll really be swellll."

When they got to the apartment Herb wished he had kept his mouth shut. But he had already offered to help this George Green and the guy would stay there and accept his hospitality with no objections. He needed this guy like he needed a headache. But here they were in the apartment and George was saying that it was a pretty nice place. Herb did not reply. He was very happy that George liked the place. Life was worth living because George liked this place. George said that he was not a restless sleeper but if Herb wanted him to he could get another cot so that they would both be comfortable. For a while it had looked as if it would be a simple thing for George to go to sleep. But he kept on talking and he started out with a violent denunciation of satin football pants, claiming that some of these halfbacks know how to slide through the line and actually slip through a man's arms because the satin slides away, and he remembered the time they were playing Duke and he had lost his temper with some little guy who came slipping through his side of the line, actually slipping through with those satin football pants. Finally he had gotten so fed up with it that he had taken a sock at the guy and had hit him. The referee had come up to him and pushed him away and then told him to get off the field. He said that he was sorry and that it wouldn't happen again, but he had to get off the field and 40,000 people booed him. It was pretty painful, he said, and the following week he did not start the Tennessee game. But in the second half they put him in and Tennessee was wearing satin football pants. But he put that out of his mind and played Big League football for the entire second half and saved a six-point lead for North Carolina when Tennessee worked the ball down to the three-yard line and—

Herb began to snore. George shut up and in a little while Herb stopped snoring and listened to hear if George was sleeping. He was. Herb wondered how long he would have to put up with this sort of thing but then, his eyes closed, he grinned and then fell asleep.

Where Herb worked the desks were gray-green wood and the

walls were gray-green. There were oblong glass bricks and straight steel fixtures. The lighting was all indirect and Herb never tired of coming in in the morning and noticing how smooth, clean, smart the offices were.

His own office was furnished with a fairly large desk, a filing cabinet, and two chairs. The chairs were gray-green steel with dark green leather seats and backs.

Helen Gillen sat in one of them now and Herb sat in his desk chair. She had come into the office with papers and for a while they had worked over the copy and account papers, research and outlines. Now they were finished with that work and Helen said that if he didn't mind she wanted to stay here for a few minutes.

She asked him to come up for dinner tonight. Norman was coming up. She would be very happy if he would accept. Norman and Ethel and Helen and Herb got along very well, and she really wanted him to come up, and would be disappointed if he said no.

"That's very kind of you," he said. He put his hand on hers, and their eyes were friendly as they smiled at each other.

When she went out of the office, he called up the apartment. It was three in the afternoon, and this George was still in bed.

"I won't be back tonight."

"You won't?"

"No, and not tomorrow morning either. You can bring your things over from the other room if you want to."

"Yes, I'll do that. When'll I see you?"

"I come back from work about six."

"All right, I'll see you tomorrow at six."

Well, he would put up with this guy for a week and then kick him out. Or maybe there was a very slight chance that he had the lug figured out wrong. If there was that chance, it was surely very slight, because if there was ever a one hundred per cent, genuine, unadulterated faker fakerissimo, it was this George Green. He put down the receiver and shook his head.

Ethel was in the kitchen exchanging pleasantries with Norman, who was reading the paper, when Herb and Helen entered.

Helen went into the kitchen to help with the dinner, and Herb started an argument with Norman over collective security. They were still arguing when dinner was ready but they stopped when the food was brought to the table, and they had to keep quiet most of the time because Ethel's swing recordings were on the radio, and, besides, Ethel had a rule that the less you talked at the table, the better your digestion. Norman said that if she was worried about his digestion she would turn off that Flat-foot Floogie with the Floy Floy and put on some soft chamber music. Ethel replied that if you looked hard enough for it, there was real beauty in Flat-foot Floogie with the Floy Floy, and Norman said that he did not feel like looking that hard for real beauty.

Afterwards Ethel suggested that there was a revival of an old favorite movie of hers playing in a neighborhood theatre, so they went there and then for a short ride and back to the apartment.

It was very cool in the living room. Ethel and Norman took the bedroom tonight, and yet the living room was just as comfortable. There was plenty of room, and two windows opened wide. Herb cupped his hands around Helen's face and she pulled him down to her, kept their lips together for a long time.

"If it wasn't somebody else it would be you."

"Likewise," murmured Herb.

"And if that somebody else didn't have another somebody else it would be me," she said.

Likewise, he said to himself.

"That's the way it goes," he said.

Enough light came in so that he could see her features very clearly yet fronted by the filmy curtain that summer night flips into a room. Eyes that looked at him sincerely when he looked at her, and closed when he kissed her, and lips and arms, her body healthy and solid beneath him. Helen solid and clean with him here in this cool room in the summer night, with the calm blanket of ethical, logical, and physiological propositions covering them both and yet not drawn tightly about them, not even touching them to make its presence felt. It let them move freely, unimpeded by bulky, useless reasoning.

In the morning they all had to get up early to go to work. In was very hot, and they took showers. Ethel was afraid of the cold water, and while she was under the lukewarm shower Norman sneaked up on her with a glass of cold water. That started a little trouble that grew until they were all throwing water and soapsuds at each other, stopping only when Helen slipped on soap and sat down very hard on the tile floor.

Before they left for work Norman said that there were some good shows being given upstate by summer stock companies and that they ought to go up some night next week. Herb had been to a few shows like this last summer. He had not liked them. But he said nothing, waiting to hear how Helen would take the suggestion. She was very enthusiastic. She wanted to go very much. So then Herb said that it was a good idea, and they all made it a definite date.

CHAPTER XVIII

What does a man like Hervey own? How much does he make a week? What are his hobbies? What does he like to do in his spare time? What kind of guy is this guy Hervey? How do you find out these things?

You know that he is out all day and he won't be back. You are alone in his apartment and so you begin to go through the closets and the bureau drawers. You don't have anything better to do. There's nothing wrong in looking through a man's bureau drawers and finding out what he owns and what he reads, what he likes in the way of ties and shirts and socks.

George opened the closet and looked at Herb's suits. He didn't like any of them. They showed no definite trend in taste and it appeared as though they were selected for Herb by the salesman. Same for the shoes. In the bureau drawers almost all the shirts were white, a few white-on-white. There were more green ties than any other color. More green socks. The guy liked green.

In another drawer there was a chest and arm exerciser, with rubber cables. With this there was a small book of directions. George took out the exerciser and idly tried it. In another drawer there was a book on selling and another on marketing. There were miscellaneous papers and diagrams. There was a memorandum notebook filled with dates for meetings and appointments, besides a few notations on what had happened and what was going to happen. These were written down obliquely, carelessly, in a loose, easy handwriting.

All the bureau drawers were used, but none were filled. The books, the socks, the underwear, were all carelessly thrown in. One drawer held nothing but a newspaper picture of "Manager Sam Mint's West City Sparrows, who took the Twilight League championship last night after a thrilling twelve-inning scrap with the Morningside Stars. Herb Hervey, fast little shortstop (third from left, third row) hit a double with two on to blow up the ball game in—"

In this same drawer there were two clippings. From the ragged edges it appeared as though they had been torn from the paper quickly. But they were not crinkled. It appeared as though they had been torn from the paper quickly in a moment of pride and perhaps joy, but that they had never left this drawer. One clipping told the story of a beautiful stop made by Herb Hervey when somebody drove a slashing liner that looked like a sure single. It went on to tell of another nice play made by Herb Hervey, a cut-off play with men on first and third. The other clipping featured Hervey as one of the outstanding infielders in the Twilight League. George read about "a fast little shortstop with plenty of zip and class. If he could hit he would go places. Manager Sam Mint says that the twenty-five-year-old Hervey is learning fast and once he gets his eye on the ball he may be Big League material. At any rate, the way this boy has been fielding thus far this season—"

Then there were some things that were thrown in haphazardly, such as a queerly shaped razor of foreign make, probably a present, a magnifying glass and compass, and then, his fingers pushing away other small articles, George grasped the barrel, ran his fingers over the muzzle, and pulled it out to look at it closely.

It was a small automatic. George examined it and then put it back in the drawer. He closed the drawer quickly and went in the other room. There were a few magazines lying around, and he picked up one and began to flip the pages. But after five minutes he got up, went back into the bedroom and opened the bureau drawer, took out the gun and put it to his head.

What are you playing around for? You know you're not gonna do it so put it back and stop acting. That's what you're doing, you're acting. I have to get it away from me, I have to put it back.

His finger moved on the trigger. He gasped and pulled his arm away. The gun was still in his hand. He shivered. The gun went back into the bureau drawer and George rushed into the bathroom and filled the washbowl with cold water. Come on, he said to himself, pull yourself out of it, pull yourself out. He ducked his head into the washbowl and kept it there for almost a minute. When he pulled it out, he looked in the mirror. He was white.

That was close, that was close, he kept saying to himself. I better get out now. I can't stay here. I better go out and find something to do because if it goes on like this I maybe I will maybe I will there's nothing to do, and it looks as though there won't be anything to do for a long time. Maybe I'm no good, maybe that's what it is. No, it isn't that, can't go telling myself that. It's just the breaks, that's what it always is, the breaks.

His own belongings, brought over from the other room the day before, were in a small closet. He selected the dark blue suit, the one he had worn that day when he had met Jean. He put it on and then stood before the mirror brushing his hair.

You don't look half bad, not half bad.

He stretched and yawned. At the door he stretched again. Going down in the elevator he yawned. It was four in the afternoon.

In town he met a few other young men his own age. Two of these young men were also out of work. But they had money. George said that he was now working and had a fairly nice apartment. The other young men suggested a party. George said why not? The other young men said why not tonight? George said why not? You got the girls? They could get girls. George gave them the address.

As on a couple other occasions in the several days he had been staying in the apartment, George had received earlier today a telephone call from Herb, who said that he would not be in tonight.

Before he parted from his friends, George said that he had no liquor at the place and he had just lost pretty heavily on the horses. He hated to do this, but he would have to ask the boys to bring their own liquor.

Five fellows and six girls came in that night and George was listening to the radio. They came in and started to make noise. In the kitchen the bottles were opened. The girls began to talk loud and laugh too loud. George was introduced to a girl named Irma. She was too small and she laughed too much. Her hair was done pageboy style and that made her look even smaller, her hair flying about small shoulders, swirling behind her small head.

No one was very funny. But they were all laughing at their own jokes and antics and to one it seemed as if all the others were having a great time. The liquor went fast and soon they were making a lot of noise and jumping around. One guy started to do acrobatics on the floor and finally came down with a hard thump. From the floor beneath there came knocks.

"Complaint department now starting in."

"Let them knock."

"Hey, less noise," said George, but he was droopy. Irma was getting on his nerves. There was too much noise. There wasn't enough noise. Irma was going over to someone else. That redheaded guy over there. Was she?

George staggered up and fell on the floor. He staggered again and took Irma away from the redheaded guy. "You stay with me."

"You like me?"

"Sure. Come on, in here with me."

"No, not yet. Please. Not yet."

He pushed her ahead of him and kicked her in the back with his knee. She fell on her face. He laughed. Irma got up and said, "What was that for?"

"Aw, can'tcha take a joke?" He turned his head for the instant and yelled, "Hey, where's that bottle'a gin I had—" and Irma hit him in the head with the telephone. He fell to his knees, dazed, and everyone was laughing. He got up laughing also, and they were all standing around, screaming laughter at him.

"Wha's so funny—what—who clipped me?" He moved about in a circle like a fighter, and then reached out and easily picked up Irma and threw her over his shoulder. She kicked her feet and tried to get at him with her fists. One of her high-heeled shoes went flying out and the heel caught one of the boys in the eye. George staggered around the room with Irma and tripped. One of the girls began fighting with her boyfriend. They stood toe to toe and called each other names as fast as they could. Another girl said that she'd get undressed if one of the boys would run out and bring back a mink coat. A fellow said, "Ron, go out and bring her a mink coat—hurry—" The guy named Ron stumbled toward the door but fell before he got to it. Then he slowly got up and went into the kitchen for another drink.

George threw Irma on the sofa. She bounced like a kitten. Someone brought George a fifth of apple brandy. It was unopened. He took off the cap and began to gurgle it down.

"Look at him, take a look at that!"

"Wow!"

He kept it to his lips, and it went down his throat.

He fell on the floor and the bottle broke, the liquor splashing on his face with the broken glass and a globe of blood coming from the lobe of his right ear.

A girl put her foot on George and pointed at him, addressing the others, who stood around. "There is your son, your flesh and blood twenty years from now. Must you bear this curse? Give to our cause and wipe the smirge the blirge the snirge of alcohol from the face of our beloved laaa-aaand—"

"My country 'tis of thee sweet land of liberty of thee I sing—"

"Aw pick him up, he's bleeding."

"That guy's so drunk we'll have to pour him back in the bottle."

"Come on, pick him up."

"Aw, leave him lay there. If he gets up again he'll get hold of another bottle and—"

"I'm all right, Coach, send me in, send me in," George said weakly.

"Sure, Coach, he's okay. He didn't cheat in the examination after all. I did. My real name is Filthy Fred and I am really not a student here at all. I was sent here by Jimmy the Jerk, who controls the West End beer territory, so's to keep good ol' George out of the ball game."

"Get that guy!"

"Lynch him!"

"Don't send me down, boys, don't send me down, cheerio, bally-o, don't send me down."

"Hey, quiet, they're banging on the wall downstairs."

"Listen," said George, "I pay rent here and—hey, I'm dyin', hey look, I'm bleeding to death—hey, will you take a look at—"

The door opened, and suddenly everyone was quiet, waiting.

Herb stood there, taking it all in. He had been having a lot of fun himself this evening. A friend of his had taken him to a penthouse gathering of three couples, and had promised much. But the blonde, who was beginning to like Herb a lot, had received a long-distance telephone call from her agent, who yelled over the wire that everything was okay, she should get on a plane right away and come out to the Coast. She started to dance and sing, leaping around the place and begging them to help her pack. The other guy said that this was all unnecessary, the packing could be done in the morning. But Herb helped her pack and she called him honey and darling. She dashed out of the place into the long black airline bus and Herb drove back to the apartment.

Now he stood there in the doorway, taking it all in.

"Wrong apartment, Mister," said one of the girls.

"What's he selling?"

The first thing Herb wanted to know was what it was all about. He ignored the damage they had done, the broken bottles on the floor, liquor spilled over the furniture, scratches on the tables, a curtain ripped and torn. First of all, he wanted to see what it was all about.

George was getting up now. He could not see straight and he did not see Herb.

"Hey, George, do you know this guy?"

Herb waited for George to recognize him.

"Oh—him." George stared, then tried to say something.

"Tell them to go home, George," said Herb. "I want to go to sleep."

"Yeah—wanna go to sleep. Tired, everybody's tired. Gotta go to sleep. C'mon." He began shoving them toward the door, nearly falling as he did so. "C'mon, tired, go to sleep, c'mon—"

"Hey, what is this, what is this?"

"C'mon—tired—"

Herb said, "This is my apartment."

"Oh, yeah? George said—"

"Never mind what George said." Herb was not angry. But he did not like this crowd, their actions, their voices, the way they looked at him. "This is my apartment."

"Well, you can be a good sport about it—"

"I don't feel like being a good sport. I'm tired, I'd like to go to sleep and so I'd like you to leave."

George was pushing them toward the door. "C'mon, it's late, c'mon—"

A few were going out, making a lot of noise and comments about Herb. But most of them were stalling, trying to antagonize him and also having fun with George. Herb could see that he was going to have trouble. One of the fellows said, "You can't do this. How do we know it's your apartment? This guy tells us to come up here and then you walk in—"

"It's my apartment, buddy. Don't let that worry you."

"I'm not letting that worry me and I'm not letting you worry me. I intend to stay here until I—"

He stopped because Herb was coming over to him. Herb had his fists clenched and ready. The guy was about five eleven, but he didn't do a thing. He let his arms remain still at his sides.

"You're a tough guy, aren't you?" he said to Herb.

There was no use wasting time trying to talk to guys like this. Herb knew that it was going to be easy. He feinted and the guy's arms went up. He hit the guy not too hard in the stomach and then bent low and picked him up in a crotch hold. He took three steps to the door and threw this guy out in the hall.

The girls started to yell and one of the fellows went for Herb and got in a few before Herb could get started. Then two more brave boys pitched in and another hopped on Herb from behind. They got him down but he was slippery and he knew what to do. He would work on one at a time. They were socking him already but he kicked one of them in the chest and another he knocked cold by bringing up his shoulder suddenly and snapping the guy's head back. George was stumbling over toward where they were fighting and Herb saw him coming. He figured that George was coming for him also. He was down and he saw George coming over toward him just before one of the fellows took slow aim and then knocked him cold while the others held him down.

Grabbing a guest, George yelled, "What's the idea?"

"He was a wise guy, wasn't he? And what's wrong with you? Come on, fellas, another wise guy."

They rushed at George. He couldn't do anything. He went down before them and they hardly touched him. He went down and fell asleep.

One of the girls came over and poured liquor on the quiet faces of Herb and George. Then the crowd left. One of the girls picked up a small quartz cigarette box that looked smart and expensive. She took it with her.

Herb was out for five minutes. He got up slowly and looked things over. His face felt wet and he looked at himself in the mirror. They hadn't done much to him. The wetness was from the liquor. There was a cut near his lip and his jaw hurt. His knuckles were bleeding.

George was breathing deeply and Herb figured that he would let him sleep for a while. In the apartment the noise of the party seemed to echo around and around from room to room. The smell of liquor was still very strong and Herb opened the windows wide. He made himself comfortable on the sofa and figured that he would get a little sleep.

He was awakened by George, who stood there unsteadily, shaking his head.

"Get out," said Herb. "Take your stuff and start moving."

"Aw, wait a minute, will ya? Give me a chance to—"

Herb got off the sofa and said, "Get out now, right now."

"Hey, let me work this off, will ya, buddy? Don't be a—"

Again Herb saw himself, held by the friends of George, and George himself coming over to help knock him cold. It was too much. He momentarily forgot what he was doing and picked up a bottle. It was broken.

"Don't—" screamed George.

Don't, Herb told himself, while he brought his arm around, and tried to pull back. But the jagged edges of the bottle ripped across George's face, tearing the nose, the lip. George screamed again, and Herb dropped the bottle. George was running crazily about the apartment, his hands to his bleeding face. The cuts were not deep, but blood ran through the fingers held up against the pain, and George ran into the bedroom, screaming and cursing Herb.

One thing was added to another. Things added up and were put into a big bag and then the bag expanded. When there was too much in the bag it blew up. The bag had just blown up. There was nothing to do now but to get even. Get even. Who was he going to get even with? Who was to blame for everything?

Before he could answer this question he had opened the bureau drawer, and had pulled out the gun.

He rushed back into the living room, and Herb said, "Put it down."

George pressed the trigger. The bullet missed Herb and swished through a chair.

"Put it down."

Swaying, trying to aim, George pointed the gun again.

Here it comes, Herb said to himself. He dodged to one side, but the gun followed him and the shot swooped low and then came up. The bullet was going in and boring through deep, burning, picking him up high and slamming him down, pressing him against the floor, then beneath the floor, then pushing the floor down on top of him.

They came and took Herb away in an ambulance. They took George to the police station. He fainted there and the doctor said that he was quite sick. One of the policemen said that he was going to be much more sick than this when he really came to and found out what he had done.

In the hospital they took the bullet from Herb's abdomen. He came to and did not know where he was. But he knew what had happened to him. All he could see about him was whiteness. A queer dark whiteness came in upon him from all sides, and there was this pain in his stomach, all through inside him. Like a cramp multiplied countless times, it persisted and each breath he took made it worse.

Two days after the shooting Herb was still in a serious condition. A few visitors came up, some from the office, including Helen Gillen, who brought Ethel and Norman along, and a few other friends. But they were not allowed in the room. Helen asked the nurse about Herb's chances, and the nurse replied that it was fifty-fifty.

It missed the front page. Most papers gave it three short paragraphs with a small two-line head. A drunken party, an argument, and one guy in the hospital and the other guy blubbering in the police station. No new angle to it, no human interest, because George Green would not explain, and no witnesses. They killed the story after the second day.

Four days after the shooting two detectives were allowed in to see Herb. He was a little improved and he could talk.

"Now he shot you after you went for him, is that it?"

"Yeah, he thought I was gonna kill him."

"Were you gonna kill him?"

"No."

"Then you mean to say he shot you in self-defense."

"That's right."

When they left, Herb closed his eyes and tried to fight back. The weakness grew on him, and he slid down, throwing up his hands weakly as it took him and carried him along with it.

Helen Gillen called up the hospital. Ethel and Norman watched her face. They saw her eyes close and her whole body tighten. They saw her lips moving, saying "Thank you," and then her hands gripping the receiver, holding it even after it was set down.

"What do they say?"

"He's very low."

Norman stood up. He wanted to say that it was a shame something like this had to happen to a guy like Herb Hervey. But if he said it, it would be just like talking about the weather. Everybody was a good fellow, a fine girl, after something like this happened to them, or after they were dead. He swallowed and sat down again.

"That's all they said?" Ethel's head was leaning to one side, her hands weakly folded in her lap.

Helen nodded.

"Well, that doesn't say—"

"It says that he's very low, Ethel," said Norman.

"Yes, but I still think—"

"Shut up," said Helen. "Just shut up." She got up and went into the kitchen and took a glass of cold water.

Ethel and Norman listened to the water running from the faucet and Ethel said, "Now what's wrong with her?"

"What do you think is wrong with her?"

Ethel shook her head and stared at the floor. She stared at Norman. Then, her head resting against her wrist, she said, "No, it isn't that. I happen to know it isn't."

Norman went into the kitchen. Helen had another glass of water to her lips.

"I'm going now. If you want to go over to the hospital, I wish you'd call me. I'd like to see him."

"That's nice of you, Norman. Thanks."

He smiled and took her hand. He let it drop. Her eyes were jumping at him. And jumping at him also was the realization that they had been alone like this only three or four times before, for certainly not more than a minute. And every time when they were alone and she looked at him her eyes jumped at him.

When something like that starts up it is very easy to stop. From now on he wouldn't walk in upon her when she was alone. Two or three months ago he might have looked into the matter for curiosity's sake, but now he and Ethel were practically engaged, and it would be Ethel from now on and only Ethel. He was sure of that because she kept popping into his mind when he woke up in the morning, and while he injected facts about protozoa and chlorophyll into the sweating heads of knowledge-hungry, knowledge-weary students. She kept popping into his mind and many times he would stop for a moment in the middle of a lecture.

All right, all right, Ethel, give me a break and scram, will you? Wait until tonight.

Then it was Ethel and only Ethel. As he walked out of the kitchen it was pretty well established. He came over to Ethel and she got up. They kissed and she said, "You're going to see me tomorrow night, aren't you?"

"Of course."

"You're going to see me every night this week, aren't you?"

"Sure."

"Do you pray, Norm?"

"No."

"Neither do I. But if you did, would you pray for Herb?"

"I think so. Yes, I would."

"You like him, don't you?"

"Yes, very much. He's straight. He's pretty swell, don't you think?"

"Sure he's swell." She closed her lips for a minute and then said, "All right, vamoose." He kissed her and left.

Ethel went into the kitchen and Helen said, "Did Norman go?"

"Don't call him Norman. You're always calling him Norman. Norm is shorter, and I don't like the sound of Norman. Norm. From now on call him Norm. Yes, he went."

He went. Meaning that he has gone. Gone. Always gone. Forever gone. Norman has gone away.

Helen walked past Ethel into the living room and Ethel followed her in.

"Look, Ethel, I don't feel like talking just now. Leave me alone for a few minutes."

"Oh, who's bothering you? Grouch." Ethel slumped down in the chair across from Helen and walled herself in with the newspaper. Slow seconds of silence followed. Then Helen came over and put her hand on Ethel's kinky blonde hair,

"I'm sorry, honey. I shouldn't be like this."

Ethel said, "Of course you shouldn't." She stopped awkwardly and in a lower voice said, "He'll be all right. And anyway—well, does he mean that much to you that you—well—"

"No. But I do like him. There's something very good about—"

"Isn't there? Norm and I were just saying the very same thing, and—"

Helen was not hearing the rest. She was in the kitchen again, alone with Norman, and she could not help it, but her eyes were looking at him, she could not stop her eyes from going at him that way. But he could. He was turning and going out, leaving her. Gone, Norman, gone away. Forever gone.

CHAPTER XIX

Dorothy turned the corner of the little block up in Harlem and walked slowly toward the tenement. Sun burst down upon the narrow street and dashed from window to window, then glowed upon the uneven bricks, flattened against the sad fronts of the tall dwellings. It seemed to have inserted itself into the air, throwing out parts of itself and allowing these tiny flames to become part of each hot globe of air that Dorothy breathed as she almost staggered down the street.

Work today had been a succession of countless separate agonies that had pressed down unmercifully on each inch of her, each fraction of each inch. She had been thinking of Tommy, and worrying about Tommy, why she had not received a letter, nothing, no news. The work pounded by with the hours, and it was something that could not be forgotten, because it hurt. Each movement, each effort hurt. And the heat magnified this hurt, broiled it down into her. Thinking of Tommy, thinking of the work, thinking of Herb, she had been subjected to one after another, passing by her, coming close, touching her, pressing, pressing hard and burning.

Herb she would probably never see again. After that night now almost two weeks ago, it was too much to expect him to come up again. It seemed to hurt him every time he was near her, and so he would stay away. Maybe he was angry with her, really angry, and no kidding. She had to smile as she walked up the steps. Herb is angry with me, she said, Herb is sore. Well, go ahead and be sore, you big sorehead.

She was so tired. So tired, so hot, so sick, so sad. No, I'm not sad. I don't want to be sad, I should never be sad. Look, I'm laughing, I'm not sad.

The hot darkness of the second-floor hallway swirled about her as she moved toward her room. When she opened the door her room was dark also, because the shades were down to keep out the sun. She pulled up the shades. She turned around and looked at the door, the floor beneath the door. A letter was there. It had a

Spanish Government postmark. It was an official letter. She picked it up and slowly tore it open.

How long ago was it that you went away? A year and a half? Two years? I'll never see you again. Never, not even your face in death. I won't see you laughing at me, I won't feel your kisses, I won't be able to touch you, to sink my fingers in your hair and pull you up against me and scream how much I hate you because you make me love you so much I love you so much love you. And you, you won't be able to touch me, to hold me. But you won't be able to miss me either. You won't be able to long for me as I must long for you. You can't even say goodbye to me, can you? Can you? Say goodbye, Tommy. Let me hear you say goodbye to me.

There seems to be a cloud before the eyes and nothing is clear. The landlady is seen and she is seen weeping and saying that she will not take the rent money, she cannot take it. But there it is, pressed into her hand, her hand being pushed away, her eyes and throat, her face moving in this weeping that cannot be heard. Then the door is open, the little street comes up against the eyes, the body turns, moves down along the street, carrying the little bag of clothes, shoes, toothbrush, letters, a few pictures, that is all.

Then the body turns again, turns a corner and walks toward the subway, a tube beneath the earth. Blasted beneath streets, so that people may ride beneath the earth. Bodies beneath the earth. Alive there. Bodies beneath the earth. Dead there.

But near the subway is a drugstore, and in this drugstore there is a phone booth. Put a nickel in the slot and call up the number that leaped around in her mind and begged to be loosed, to run down through her arm to her fingertips, to be dialed so that he would talk to her.

If you need me you know where to call me.

I need you.

Then call me.

The nickel went into the slot, the fingers dialed, the ringing started at the other end of the wire. Once, twice, three, four. How many times must a phone ring? Twelve, thirteen. Please answer, won't you answer please? About twenty now, twenty-one, twenty-two. Not home. Won't answer. Maybe it's better that you don't answer. Yes, it is better.

The body must act, the feet must walk. To be still is to increase the pain. Things must be done, attended to, actions must be taken. But now there is no place to go, nothing to do. Everything has already happened, nothing else can happen. It's all over.

Yet she was getting into the subway and it was taking her across the city. She was getting out of the subway and walking up the steps to a wide street that separated rows of tall houses, with polished brass door knobs and heavy brownstone fronts, clean, rounded glistening windows, trimmed shrubbery and dark red, orange, purple flowers. Clean wide streets separating these rows of tall, darkly rich homes.

To one of these homes Dorothy came with steps that seemed to be separate journeys, each one. It took too long to get here. A lifetime had been spent away from this home, another lifetime was being passed walking up the steps, ringing the bell.

"Of course we'll take you back. You're making me feel terrible talking like that. You're still our child, Dorothy. You made a mistake, but we must all forget about that. You'll start over again, dear. We'll make believe you just graduated from college again and now you're starting out, planning a course. You must get in touch with your old friends, and do the things you used to do, before you— Well, we'll start right in. Tomorrow we'll—"

The father patted his daughter's head while the mother talked on. Then the father began, and he said that it would be a simple matter to get Dorothy a temporary job so she could take up her time actually working and getting her mind off things.

Then later in the evening a sister came in and a brother, another sister. There was a lot of talk. One of the sisters cried. The brother tried hard to make Dorothy blend in with his mood, which was It's-all-over-so-let's-start-to-laugh-and-sing. They were all trying hard to help her. Upstairs her old room was clean and big. Her mother began pointing out the arrangement of chairs and dresser, mirrors and bed, just as Dorothy had left this room nearly three years ago.

They were all talking except Dorothy. She listened to each one as they talked, and tried to appear attentive. She tried hard to smile, to act as they wanted her to act. And then at last she was going up the stairs and saying good night. She was going to sleep and in the morning she would get up and here she would be, in her parents' house, with her sisters, her brother. It would be this way, then. Going in town with Mother. Meeting a few of the girls. Meeting more of the girls. Dad, getting her an easy job. The girls, the fellows. The tall, the short gooks calling for her once more. Tall and short, white tie, tails, patent-leather dancing pumps. Perfume and flowers, a shining floor and dripping melody. The memory of her debutante days.

Once more then, back again where she had been, taking up again where she had left off. Things to do and people to meet. This house now, with her parents and her sisters and her brother. Back again. Dorothy was back home again.

Her eyes stared at nothing except the darkness of the room and the faint outlines of wood and glass against the thick dark blue oozing in through the open window. Her eyes slowly closed, her breathing deepened, memory and longing faded in the darkness.

CHAPTER XX

When the doctor came to the bedside, Herb's eyes were open. He looked up and said, "It looks pretty good, doesn't it?"

The doctor wanted to grin. But he allowed a frown to play about his eyes, and said, "Do you feel pain?"

"Plenty."

"That's all right."

"Sure. It's swell. I love it." Herb moved about by inches.

He saw the doctor leaving the bedside, and then the nurse came over and put a thermometer in Herb's mouth. When she took it out, Herb said, "What do you read?"

He tried to imitate a newsboy, but his voice was still weak. "You're coming down," said the nurse.

"I guess I'll be out of here by tomorrow then."

"Oh, sure. First thing in the morning. We'll make you get dressed and kick you right out the front door."

"No kidding, how long do you think I'll be honoring this place with my presence?"

The nurse said, "If you keep up the good work we'll send you home in two weeks."

"My lucky summer," said Herb. He sighed and grinned at the nurse.

She went out and came back in a few minutes. "Do you feel like seeing anybody?" she said.

"If it's the cops again tell them I'm sleeping. When they do come they don't even bring flowers—"

"It's not the cops. It's the nice lady who sent you those carnations."

Helen came in. Herb grinned at her. His eyes were still bright from sickness and fever, his face pale from pain and weakness.

"Hello."

"Hello," she said. Her face gladdened at his grinning lips and eyes.

"And how are you?"

"Fine, thanks, Herb. How are—"

"Oh, I'm doing wonderful. I just got finished a fast game of handball before you came in. They make me run two miles every morning. I'm doing great. How do I look? That's a dumb question, isn't it?"

"No. You look very much alive."

"You've been here a lot, haven't you, Helen?"

"Well, a few times."

"And you sent me those, didn't you?" He looked toward the flowers. "Do you like carnations?"

"Crazy about them. For years I've been wishing I could get real sick and be sent to a hospital so some kind lady would send me carnations. How are they getting on at the office without me?"

"Very poorly. Your accounts are from malnutrition."

"I suppose that without me around things are practically at a standstill."

"It's nice and cool in here," said Helen. She looked around the room.

"Oh, it's great. I enjoy every minute of it."

"I'm glad you're being disagreeable," said Helen. "That's a good sign. It shows that your resistance is stronger. You're probably very cranky right now, aren't you, driving the nurses crazy."

"Who's cranky?"

"Men usually are when they're sick in bed."

"I'm not cranky." The nurse came in. "Am I cranky, Miss Denton?"

"No, you're a very good patient." To Helen she said, "He is, he's very nice."

Helen nodded. I know he is.

After she left, Herb thought about her for a while but then his mind switched off and he thought of someone else. He could not get his mind on any one subject for more than a few minutes at a time, because this other party broke in and dominated his thoughts. Trying not to think of her only made it worse. The only way to stop it was to sleep. Even then she was there, because when he awoke she was right with him, all the time with him.

Blood keeps on coursing through the body, air is taken in, food is taken in, the machine keeps on running. Torn tissues are mended, glued, nailed, spliced, inserted together again and this healing keeps up, going slowly ahead until the time comes when the mind knows that there is no more hurt, there is the lightness and the relaxed, flowing, somewhat delightful feeling of health once more.

Days pass slowly but then more quickly as one sits up, finally gets up, then puts on a shirt, a tie, a pair of shoes.

He walked out of the hospital. It was really remarkable, he thought. He could walk and he felt like walking. He watched his feet moving on the ground.

Helen was beside him. She held him back and said, "Not so fast."

They got in the taxi and at his apartment she said, "You'll need someone here. You can't manage yourself."

"That's right."

"Well—"

"I'll call up for a nurse."

"No. I'll stay with you."

"Oh, no, I won't have you going to all that trouble—"

"Please, Herb. I'd rather. You see, Ethel and Norman are engaged now. They might as well stay at the apartment together. They'll probably be married within a month. I'd have to find a new place anyway. So—well, that is, if you don't mind me staying here—"

"Do you think I mind?"

"No, I don't."

She moved in with him. Ethel and Norman came over that night and celebrated his recovery. They were sitting around, laughing, and Herb was in good form with his dry side remarks. The phone rang, and someone was downstairs. He wanted to see Herb.

"It's George Green."

"Oh."

"May I come up?"

"I have company."

"I don't care. Please, I just want to say a few things and then I'll leave. I won't be long."

He came up, and when Herb started to introduce him he said, "Please, these people don't want to know me. What do they want to know me for? What good can I do them? What good did I do you? Anybody? What good did I do myself?"

George did not look good. He had lost a lot of weight. He was clean, his hair was well-brushed, his suit was pressed, he did not need a shave. But he did not look good.

He said, "I'm out on bail now. If you decide not to prosecute, I'll be discharged."

"I'm not pressing any charges."

"All right. Thanks. I—don't suppose I'll ever be in a position to make up for what I've done. But if I ever can, you have my word now. You probably realize that I didn't mean to do it."

Herb had to smile. He thought of two little kids fighting in the street, and one kid hitting the other in the head with a rock and then crying that he didn't mean to do it.

"I guess it sounds funny to you," said. George.

"A little. If you could come over and knock me cold while your friends held my arms, you could also—"

"Wait. You'll have to take my word for this. When they had you down I was coming over to help you. But I couldn't do anything. All they had to do was push me. Then, of course, later, when you took a swing at me with that bottle, I lost my head and—there's no use going over it. I was fully to blame, and it was only tonight that I got myself together enough to come up and—listen, I'll go now, and I hope you believe me, anyway, partly believe me."

Herb said, "Yes, I believe you. It's okay." He put out his hand.

"No," said George, "I can't do that. Somehow I can't."

"Come on." Herb kept his hand outstretched. George took it. But he could not look Herb in the face.

"Good luck."

The door closed and they could hear George slowly walking down the hall. Helen, Ethel and Norman looked at each other and then at Herb. He said, "Now if we had a band here they'd sit down and play 'My Buddy,' and then a little white-haired lady would come in and the handkerchiefs would have a field day and I'd find out that he was my long-lost brother, just returned from thirty years' watermelon farming in the Ozarks."

He grinned, but the others did not. The grin was lost from his face. He wondered why they looked at him like this. Then they were looking at each other and then looking back at him. He wondered why. He did not see the admiration in their eyes, mainly because he was not looking for it.

CHAPTER XXI

Some days just about manage to hobble by. They even seem to stop and rest for a while, and then continue on, dismally groping ahead and finally fading away. Some days pass like a streak. Some months pass like a streak. There is no change of pace. Each day whizzes up to the plate and is smashed away to a memory, and each day is fast, too fast.

Yet each day was somewhat comforting, because after a while he was able to work, and then he could get around easily, and he could enjoy things, he could eat and digest without discomfort, and then he could forget about his hurt, because there was so much to do.

These days whizzed by, and he worked hard, not letting up, working not only because he had to put in so many hours each day, for which he would be paid so many dollars at the end of the week, but because he enjoyed the work. The problems, the single troubles, the process of creating an idea, discarding, combining, and finally examining the result, putting it up for inspection, now had a fascination heretofore nonexistent.

There was this hard work, then, eight hours a day, and afterwards he and Helen would drive back to the apartment, and go out to eat, then do something. They made it a point to do something every night. They would go out with Ethel and Norman. They would drive to the beach, go to a summer theater upstate, they would go to a concert, or they would visit a few of his or her friends. They would see a lot of movies and hear a lot of music.

Living well like this, they spent a lot of money. But it was a smooth flow of spending, and it was not motivated by a desire to get rid of money merely for the sake of spending, but because they truly desired to do these things, visit places, see things and people, and do it quietly, evenly, so that it soon became an established schedule.

But it was not enough. All this is well and good, Herb would tell himself, and the longer it keeps up, the better. Yet no matter how long it keeps up, no matter what happens, I'll still find myself waking up at night and seeing Dorothy, I'll still find myself at times wanting to see her. One day he decided that he just had to see her.

The landlady in the Harlem tenement saw him coming up the steps one day in late August, and she wondered where he had been all this time. She shook her head as soon as he came up to her.

"She didn't leave no address," said the landlady.

"Nothing at all?"

"I don't know what she's done or where she's went. But I do know this. She went away because something terrible happened. Maybe if you'd been around you'd know what it was." The landlady seemed to be accusing him, and he wondered why he should feel so guilty now.

Lamely he was saying, "I've been sick, that's why I couldn't come up here." He wanted to say this to Dorothy. That's why I've been away. I've been sick, Dorothy.

"Well, she got this letter from Spain tellin' her the bad news, and right after—"

"The bad news."

"Yeah, I don't need to tell ya. Her husband. He—"

Herb said, "You don't have any idea where she went."

"No."

"But look— I gave her my address. She knew where to call me. Why didn't she call me?"

"Now how can I answer that?" The landlady moved backwards, inside the doorway, and Herb backed down the steps.

Why didn't you call me? Why didn't you come to see me? You couldn't find me? You should have hunted through every street, every inch of the city until you found me. You didn't want to find me. You didn't want to.

Helen was reading when Herb walked in. He saw her look up and then quickly lower her eyes to the book again. He sat down and picked up the newspaper. But then he had put it down and was staring at the floor. Helen looked at him from the side of the book. After a while she put the book down.

She didn't say anything, but he was conscious of her glance. He looked up.

"I lied to you before," he said. "I told you I was going out to see my lawyer, and arrange divorce proceedings with Jean. I didn't do that. I went someplace else."

"You don't have to tell me where, Herb."

"You know?"

"No."

"I never wanted you to know. But I should tell you. I should have told you long ago. Now I will tell you."

He told her. Briefly, truthfully, he told her everything. Finally he could only shrug and say, "I guess it's all over."

Helen was not saying a word. She was gazing at him and then she was looking away, and then gazing at him again.

He wondered why Helen was not saying anything, and he asked her with his eyes.

She said, "You'll find her, Herb."

"I don't think she wants me to find her."

"But could you find her?"

"I don't know where to look."

"You'll try, though."

"No, Helen, I won't try. It's probably all over now, it's—" She doesn't even know I'm alive, all she knows now is that he's dead. Oh, you poor kid, where are you, what's happened to you?

"Is that the way you really feel about it, that it's all over?"

"Yes."

"Then you'll have to do something about that, Herb. You'll have to stop thinking about it."

"Sure."

"But that's a dumb suggestion, isn't it?" She smiled at him.

"No. Any time you catch me acting as if someone just hit me in the head with a flowerpot, snap me out of it. Throw cold water on me."

"And vice versa."

"What?"

"You heard me."

"Oh." He stood up, and came over to her. Her smile widened to a grin. Then he grinned. Each knew that the other was forcing it now, but it was all right. After a while their grins changed to expressions of placid enjoyment.

She threw cold water on him a few times. Once, to get him out of it, she slapped him hard across the mouth, and then was so sorry that she fell into a mood herself, and he crept up on her and threw a full glass of cold water in her face.

Late one night Helen awoke to find him sitting up in bed, looking out the window.

His hair was ruffled, falling over his forehead. She looked up at him and could see his face fully. He was staring out the window, and a slice of light caught the side of his face, forcing a glow into his eyes. He looked like a little boy staring out at the night sky and wondering what was up there.

Helen closed her eyes. She felt like turning over on her side now, but the noise would probably disturb him. She remained still, and presently he lay down and soon was sleeping. His arm stretched out and touched her forehead. Helen did not draw away. His hand was cool and soothing on her brow.

CHAPTER XXII

In Wilda's apartment Herb waited while she went into the other room to get the letter. It was the first letter since Paul and Jean had gone away together. Wilda had called up excitedly and now Herb wondered what Paul had to say.

It was middle August now. Three months ago Paul and Wilda had been together, he and Jean had been together. He nearly laughed aloud when he thought that. He and Jean had been together. That was really funny.

Misery and waiting had brought a plaintive beauty to Wilda. She came in now from the other room and Herb could see that she was living quietly, waiting, wondering in a matter-of-fact way how long it would be until Paul would realize what he had done. There were no lines of hardship on her face. Her eyes were clear, her cheeks were full. She had even gained weight. And now she came in from the other room and she was smiling.

"Read this."

The letter was from China. Herb looked up and said, "They're getting around."

"Just read it."

Paul's handwriting was even, but there were sentences which seemed to tremble. This was one of the first things that Herb noticed.

"Dear Wilda:

The reason I waited this long before writing you was that I did not want to write any lies. I wanted to be sure of everything before putting it down on paper. Now you and Herb must believe me, and I want you to show this letter to Herb. I know you will both believe me. Jean does not know that I am writing this. She did not want me to write at all. She expects to be coming back soon but I know differently. We will not be back for a long time. I am very busy over here now, although as yet I am not flying much. I have a ground job right now. But still Jean doesn't like it here and she wants to get back. We had a big argument about it last night. That is one of the reasons I am writing today. I didn't want to write, but Jean is not around now, and she did not have much to say this morning. I felt that I had to say something to somebody and I also felt that there were a lot of things you must know.

"By this time you probably have decided that you will get a divorce and Herb has decided the same thing. Of course you will not have any trouble financially, but if you do need extra money, you won't have any trouble making a settlement with my lawyer.

"Jean and I fell in love and we had to go away together. That is all I can tell you. I want to tell you more but I can't. Some day we will see each other and I will tell you everything.

"This war might last for another year, it might last for ten years. The way things are going now I would say that it might last forever. This is really a war. There is no question about that.

"Please do not write, because I don't want Jean to know that I have written you. I will write again soon...."

In the last two paragraphs he practically repeated himself and then he closed the letter in trembling handwriting.

Herb looked up and Wilda said, "What do you think of that?"

"He ought to learn how to write a letter."

"But what do you think of it?"

"He's none too happy."

"Do you know what I'm going to do?"

Somehow he guessed it even before she told him. She said that she was going to him. When she said that her eyes flamed, as if she were preparing a crusade.

"He needs me. Every word he wrote in this letter tells me that. And I'm going to him right away. I'm not wasting a minute. She took him away from me but now I'm going to get him back. He didn't want to go away with her. He's sorry now. Can't you see that? He doesn't have to write it. You can tell by the way he—"

"It looks that way. She roped him in."

Wilda said, "You better go now, Herb. I'm going to pack. If you stay around I'll only waste time talking. China's a long distance away, and I'm in a hurry."

First the artillery begins on them. The artillery pounds away and does not stop until the ground and the buildings and the flesh are ploughed into a broiling, formless heap of ruin. In and around this mass the bodies somehow move about, orders are given, men still live. They get back into position, the reserves come up and the line of defense is stretched taut once more. But then the planes come. They move high and in front of the creeping infantry which must mop up after the strafing is completed, and which must occupy the new position. The planes bomb, they strafe, and sometimes they meet the planes of the enemy, sent over in a desperate attempt to delay the attack.

The artillery had stopped, and now the Chinese forces saw the planes coming over. It seemed that there were hundreds of dots in the sky moving steadily toward them. The dots grew larger and the wings, the wheels were visible. There were about fifty Japanese planes. They were coming now, very fast.

This battle had been foreseen weeks in advance. It had important geographical aspects. The ground must be held, there must be no retreat. The Chinese had an advantage in manpower here, and the order was emphasized, no retreat.

But the bombardment had done a lot of damage. The screams and groans increased along the line and were mingled with the rising moan of fear as the planes came nearer. Men imprisoned in this line of trenches looked back instead of forward.

Some of them, looking back, saw dots in the sky coming from the other direction. And these dots, like the others, took on definite form. The cries suddenly inverted from hopelessness and fear to joy and hope. The Chinese planes swooped and moved in dogged formation, aiming at the enemy. The two groups would meet just above the Chinese lines.

As they met, the orders on the ground below came swift and harsh. Already the Japanese infantry was advancing, at a pace much more slow than that called for by the original battle plans. The Chinese made ready.

In the air, almost a hundred planes whirled about like maddened birds. Bombers lumbered ahead, while pursuit planes desperately circled about to keep off the light, wicked spurting Chinese two-seaters. The air became heavy with smoke and fumes of gas and oil, bullets lining through the clouds, and through all this the deafening buzz and screeching, then roaring, then whining sounds of the motors, cut thickly by the clicking guns.

Among the Chinese fliers there were some who knew what the bombers could and could not do. They knew what the Japanese pursuit planes were capable of, and they knew their own potentialities. They cut under, swooped above, shot down three bombers in less than ten minutes. The Japanese planes were scattered. Then another bomber was shot down. There were only three left. At these the enemy charged, from above, from beneath, forcing the smaller guarding craft to protect themselves. And then one bomber suddenly split in two, seeming to stop for a moment, then dropping straight to the battleground beneath like a broken rock.

Planes were dropping now, men were falling among the flames and smoke, the sky was streaked and shot through with red and gold, yellow and smoke-lined orange as engines burst, guns sprayed bullets into gasoline tanks, blood ran over the sides of cockpits.

Still the Chinese planes dipped and moved ahead, more came on, the leaders dove, came up and behind the small pursuit models that now had no bombers to guard. And then slowly at first, faster as the advantage was followed up and realization of defeat spread among the Japanese, they started back. They raced and zigzagged, dipped and rose, trying to get away from the pursuing guns. But many were shot down. From a defeat it became chaos. They were almost completely wiped out of the sky.

The victors in this air battle now concentrated their attention on the ground. Waves of Japanese infantry were advancing toward the first Chinese positions. At a few points they had reached the trenches and there were already several spots where hand-to-hand bayonet fighting was taking place. Acting on their own initiative, coupled with optional orders given in sham battles, the Chinese flew low over the charging attackers, strafed them, then kept on going, and finally discovered what to them was a simple problem in air maneuvers.

They discovered motorized equipment, armored cars and small trucks, larger trucks, rushing troops up to the front line. They attacked. Their bombers loosed projectiles onto the thin moving line, and the fliers looked down, saw explosions in the midst of this line, and then saw the line broken up. They kept on going, bombing, their machine guns clicking away steadily, following up the advantage.

And finally the line turned back. The reserves made their retreat, a quick retreat necessitated by the possibility of an almost immediate counterattack. The Chinese planes kept after the retreating army. Annihilation grew until men tried to bury, to almost drown themselves in rice swamps, trying to get away from the bombs and the bullets.

Up ahead the Japanese surrendered. They were hedged in quickly, their ranks broken. They had to surrender. Coming back, the Chinese fliers looked down and saw the prisoners massed in quiet formation, already being taken back. The fliers signaled to each other. It had been a great day.

The planes landed and from one of them, a bomber, Paul Schuen, got out. Slowly he took off his leather helmet and goggles. His face was shining wetly with grease and sweat. His suede jacket was covered with blood. Part of this was his own, from a shoulder wound. Most of it was from the bullet-smashed chest of another American, whose body they were now removing from the big plane.

Paul shook his head to get his senses together and fight off the dizziness that was now moving in upon him. Another American came over.

"They get you?"

"In the shoulder," said Paul. "We didn't do half bad, did we?"

"Hey, look at that. They got Chris."

"They got him right, didn't they?" Paul looked down at the body, now being lifted, now being taken away. "He would've made a couple grand out of this."

"Come on, we'll fix up your shoulder." The other American was beckoning to a Chinese ambulance driver.

It was late when he entered the room. Jean was sleeping. He tiptoed across to the bathroom and made faces as the throbbing in his shoulder became more and more annoying. There was a funny taste in his mouth and he gargled with water. When he spit it out a tooth and blood came with the water. Then he looked down at his hands. There were cuts in his fingers, and a deep gash in his wrist. When a man fights he has to expect these things, Paul told himself, and it is only afterwards when he looks at himself and begins to count up that he finds out how much you can hurt yourself when you fight. The blood ran from his wrist. Yes, he told himself, if you fight you must expect to get hurt.

Through the blinds yellow light began to seep into the other room. Jean rested on her stomach, one arm bent beneath her face. Paul walked into the room and stood there wondering whether to go to sleep or to write her a note saying he would fly back to the hangar and spend the rest of the day there. But just then she awoke. She sat up quickly, throwing back her hair, staring at him.

"What—what—wha—"

"Go back to sleep," he said.

"Your shoulder—what happened?" But she did not get out of the low bed.

"Scratch. Just grazed. It's nothing."

"You were fighting?"

"No. Little accident over at the hangar."

She looked at the blinds, pulled them up and peered outside. "It's still early," she said.

"Yeah. Go back to sleep. I'm going back to the hangar. I'll be away all day."

"But you've been away for two days already, and you said—"

"I can't help it, Jean. It's my job. I'm not playing around. I have to work." It had really been three days, not two.

"I'll go with you."

"No, no. Now please stop that, Jean. You know I can't take you to the hangar. In the first place I'm not allowed, and—"

"Listen." She bit her lip and her hand shook as it rubbed down her cheek. "I want to go back. I really want to go back home. I don't want to stay here. I don't want to have my baby here. We're going back."

For a moment he could not answer her. There was pain in her eyes and her lips moved now, saying nothing. She was sitting up in the bed, and there was hurt within her. But she did not plead. She was ordering him to take her back home.

"There's no good reason—" he began.

"There's every good reason. Do you realize where we are? We're in China."

"Well?" He had to grin. The way she said it made him grin.

"It's funny, isn't it?" Bitterness.

"Wait, Jean." Before he said another word it came to him that she was examining him. Her eyes were moving in quick spurts from his shoulder to his face, still marked from grease, from wind cutting at it, and the whiteness around his eyes, protected by the goggles. Then too, his hands, cut, the bloody mark on his wrist. Maybe she was also noticing the rip in his jacket, and perhaps she could perceive a certain tenseness in his manner, the impression given off by one who has just been in a battle. But then he said, "You're not having it bad here. I think we're situated pretty nicely. You got friends, haven't you?"

"Oh, loads of them." She pushed more bitterness into her voice.

"But you feel all right?"

"No, I don't. I'm sick. And I'll get sicker yet if you don't take me home."

"Let me get something straight. Just what do you mean by home?"

"What do I mean by home," she mimicked him. "The South Pole."

"We've had this out before, but once and for all we might as well settle it now. You're going to have a baby within two months. If we go back now I have to marry you right away. But I can't marry you without a divorce from Wilda. And you're still married to Herb. How do you know they'll be willing to help us out?"

"I want to go home," she said doggedly, not looking at him.

"And then you—"

"I want to go home, I want to go home," she said.

"Jean—"

"I want to go home, I want to go home—"

"Jean—"

"Leave me alone, I want to go home." She burst out in a wild shriek. "Take me home!" She fell down on the bed, breathing hard but not sobbing.

She's putting on an act. She did this once before. She'll do it again. It's not good for her, with the kid in her, she better stop getting herself excited.

Paul went over and sat down beside her. He patted her head and kissed her trembling cheek. "This doesn't do you any good, Jean. You mustn't get yourself excited. Now we'll—"

"Take me home, take me home."

"Stop that, will you?"

"Take me home."

"How can I take you home, how can I?" He got off the bed and then closed his eyes as the throbbing in his shoulder deepened to a sudden angry pain. His hands went up to his eyes and he tried to shake it off. Hopelessness and self-pity overcame him in this moment and he let out a wavering sob.

Forcing away this threat of a breakdown he again came over to the bed and said quietly, "Go back to sleep, Jean. We'll talk it over later."

"Take me home, take me home," she moaned, her eyes closed.

Paul went into the other room and got undressed. His shoulder was thickly bandaged and at the infirmary they had told him not to stay on his feet too much, because he might strain the wound and bleeding might start. He looked at the bandage and expected to see blood seeping through. But there was no blood, only the whiteness of the bandage.

Maybe it will bleed, he thought. He didn't care. So if it would bleed it would bleed. He was extremely tired now. Half undressed he slid low on the lounge and forgot everything.

In the other room Jean kept on moaning, "Take me home, take me home." At last she was sure that Paul could not hear her. She got up slowly, and softly made her way across the reddish straw rug to the wide opening of the next room. The thick yellow light flowed in a slow mass through the open window, and she could see the glaring beams settle on Paul's face, igniting his short, wavy hair with snaky sparks.

His broad chest went up and down slowly, and the rest of him was very still. His booted legs were stretched out wearily across the matted rug, and his heavy arms hung over the side of the orange reed lounge chair.

Jean went over to the chair and looked down at the bandaged shoulder. It was a thick bandage. He had said it was just a scratch. An accident at the hangar. She picked up the suede jacket from the floor. There. A hole through the shoulder. Now, the silk shirt he had worn beneath the jacket, where was it? Over there, where he had thrown it before lying down. She picked it up and saw another hole. A scratch? There was blood in almost a perfect circle around the hole in the silk shirt. There was a black rim to this ring of blood.

She ran her eyes up and down him. His wrist, it was bleeding even now, and his fingers were bleeding, they were cut, one of them looked very badly cut.

You're hurt, then, aren't you? You've been fighting, haven't you been fighting? You've been shot because you were fighting. That's why you have that bandage there. They shot you because you were fighting them. Because we're here, because you wanted to come here, that's why you're shot, bleeding, hurt there now. Won't you be good to me and stop this? I don't care where you take me now, I only want to get away from here, where you fight and get shot, bleeding. Wrist bleeding. Hurt. You're hurt. Because you were fighting.

Far in the distance, to the north, there started a low booming, which was so faint at first that it blended into the silence. Then it assumed a defiant independence, set itself off apart from other sounds, and kept up, a low booming.

Paul opened his eyes. At first he did not see Jean standing there, watching him. He had his eyes opened in a surprised stare, and he heard this low booming, which had awakened him.

Slowly he got up, and he saw Jean. "Cannon," he said. "Near here. I don't understand it."

"Cannon?"

"Listen," he said, more to himself than to her. He was merely voicing his thoughts aloud. He was not speaking to Jean.

"Why—that's shooting, isn't it? That's—the war," she said.

"You wait here, Jean," he said, as if he thought that she would not wait. "I have to make a telephone call."

He slowly put on his shirt and suede jacket, and went out of the apartment. Jean sat down, listening to the low booming to the north.

This was the war, then, and it was near enough for her to hear. The guns were shooting now, and men were fighting. It was the war, and it was very near. She could hear men fighting. And now, if this sound of fighting were near enough to hear, it meant that they had come from some place more distant, and coming, they approached. Approach meaning to come nearer, there was only one conclusion. The war was coming here. Someone was being shoved back, and someone was moving forward.

Then the war was coming here, where she was, where Paul had assured her so many times that she would be safe.

Where had he gone? What was he doing now? A telephone call. Why did he have to make a telephone call? Why was he not here with her now, when she was so afraid, when she was afraid and in pain, with the baby hurting her, inside of her, giving her pain.

Paul was coming up the steps, trying to run. He was in a hurry, then. She met him in the doorway and he moved past her and said, "I have to be going."

"What's the matter?"

"I'm needed up ahead."

"You can't go—"

"Where's my—"

"You're not going!"

He faced her and said, "No matter what happens, I want you to stay here. Don't leave the apartment. You stay here, Jean. I don't think I'll be away long. But if I am, don't you worry. I have to go now. Don't worry."

He bent down to kiss her, but she pushed him away, her head bent to one side. A moment's mask of pain crossed his face, and then he left.

Then he was going up ahead to where the guns boomed, back to the fighting that was pushing someone back, and she was to stay here alone, and not to leave this place. She was to stay here and just stay, do nothing but stay and wait until he should come back from the fighting.

She rang for the servant, and asked for something to eat. The servant brought toast and tea. Jean took two bites and a sip and could do nothing more. Yet she was hungry. The toast and tea were there before her and she was hungry but she could not eat.

The guns boomed, and she listened. Were they louder now?

Why, yes, they were louder. They were actually louder. Well, they were louder, that was all. The guns were louder. No, it meant something else. They were nearer.

She stood tense, her clenched fists like rock against her chin.

She remained like this for some time. Then, very weak, almost cloaked in a cloud of dizzy fog, she stumbled over to the couch, and collapsed on the silk cushions.

There were many like her in this settlement, on the outskirts of the Chinese river city. They huddled together and tried to deafen themselves to the sounds of fighting, which now were louder. There were messages and phone calls, and then telephone communication was cut off entirely, the electric lights went out, a snapping silence followed, and then the eyes were wide, the mouths moving slowly, questioning, What is wrong, What has happened?

Fear grew and covered the small houses, the sampans on the river, the apartment houses in the foreign settlement, and the guns, the booming, grew louder. Into the yellow sky great flurries of smoke leaped and twisted, then became gray masses into which were hurled fiery spheres, spreading out in white puffs. The frightened eyes looked up at this and wondered what it was, at the same time knowing, yet not ceasing to wonder.

On the street people moved like ants threatened with rainfall. The thunder of metal and the shriek of split air came rushing down and pushing, jerking, pulling people about, throwing several to the ground, causing a few to yell like scared children. And finally the germ of panic multiplied itself, and the people began to run. Almost at the same time a siren sounded, and another siren sounded.

Coming toward this city on the river, flying high, were seven bombers. They were acting as an accompaniment to a surprise attack facilitated by a sudden fastening of railroad lines, thus closing a gap and allowing a speedy movement of troops to a sector virtually abandoned by the Chinese. The enemy rushed troops and guns up along this line, pushed forward and were even now pushing forward and meeting practically no resistance. And now, to further the effect of shock and surprise, they had loosed the bombers, whose mission it was to smash the supply and transportation bases nearest to the point of attack. These supply bases, railroad stations, and two munitions factories were in and around the city on the river.

Screaming together, the sirens and people whirred their yells of fright as the bombers approached. And finally the cords of human grouping were loosened, and each man, woman, child, was a single creature moving with but one purpose, his own preservation.

From above, the objectives were not quite clear. There was the river, there was the city, and there, far to the left, was a railroad. The bombers came on. The first projectile was sent down. It hit a patch of uncultivated field. Even before it dropped another went down. Another. The planes passed on, turned, came back, the bombs went down.

The Japanese fliers were only partly successful. They could only see mass damage. They had destroyed the railroad station, the low, wide buildings which had been designated as supply dumps, and another structure on the river bank. But they could not see the other destruction, the wrecked houses, the two four-story apartment houses, smashed and split, with bricks and blood falling together into the crumbled street.

Something comes crashing down on top of you, but then slips to the side and brings down things from all other sides, hitting up against you, carrying you down with it. Something pins you against a wall, drags you away, flips you out like a leaf in the wind and drops you to the ground, then hammers you into a dark room, drags you out and places you in a white room, where you open and shut your eyes and see people in white go by, and hear noise, moans, shrieks, bells, dragging feet. You hear your own groans, your own cries, then you hear nothing but your own coughing and choking as you try to drag air down into lungs that are punctured, down into a body already torn and broken.

Sounds of low speech slowly rising rolled in from the hospital corridor, and she heard his voice, and then the doctor's, and then his voice again.

"... see her."

"Serious ... shock ..."

"... hope?"

"... afraid not."

The head, the short, dark brown curly hair, his face, the suede jacket and that hole in the shoulder, his eyes looking at her as he came into the room. Then Paul was here with her.

It sounded funny to her, the way she said it. She said, "See?" like a housewife who has fallen down the stairs after repeatedly warning her husband to fix that top step.

"See?" she said, in a gasping whisper.

He wanted to kiss her, and bent down over the bed.

"No," she said. Her voice was stronger now.

"I shouldn't have gone away without you. I should have taken you with me. How could I have done it, though? But I shouldn't have left you there."

"See?" Her eyes cursed him.

"You aren't seriously hurt, you're—"

"Oh, no? I'm dying. I can feel it. You can't feel it. You can look at me and tell me I'm not hurt. It's easy for you to say that. But I can feel it, and it does hurt, and I know what's happening to me. I'm dying."

"I shouldn't have—"

"You didn't care. It didn't make any difference to you. And it won't make any difference after—"

She was leaving him, then. The words were confused, entangled, and he could not get them out. I love you, Jean. Why did I bring you here? Why did I take you away from him and bring you here? I loved you. I love you now. Do I love you now? Can I say that I love you now, when you are going away from me? Do you want me to tell you that? Do I still love you? Do you, do you love her? She's going now.

"Paul—Paul—" She started to breathe fast, and tried to draw her shaking arms from beneath the covers.

"Easy—"

"Paul—is it—now? Is this the way it is? Like this? Like—like when it gets so dark that I can't see anymore but my eyes are open. I know, because I can feel that they're open but I can't see you and here it—look, just like a train, I can see it coming—Paul—look—" She wanted to say something and it was choking her. "Listen—please—I—"

Now her eyes were closed and her lips were closing also. She was relaxing, but there was still the evidence of effort. She was fighting to tell him something.

Then it came again, from lips nearly closed. He bent down low, straining to hear as she murmured, "The baby—I'm sure now, something tells me—for sure. Yes, I do know now—it's not yours. It's Herb's. The baby belongs to Herb and me. Herb and me. Just ours—our baby—where is our baby? Where is Herb? What happened? Tell me what happened? I want to—know, because I—Wilda will—will—be—"

Her lips were still. Her eyes were closed. It was all over. The doctor came into the room. Paul looked down at the white face and said to the doctor, "She was going to have a baby."

"Yes." But the doctor did not say what was in his mind, that if it had not been for the baby within her, she would have lived. He looked at Paul and then his arms shot out and he held this falling man, then gripped him under the arms and called for a nurse.

At first they thought that he had fainted from the shock, but when they took off his jacket, they saw the blood welling out into the thick bandages around his shoulder.

Three American aviators were standing at the hotel bar, bent earnestly over their glasses, when one looked in the bar mirror and saw her coming in through the bronze and green enamel door.

"That's smart."

"Yeah, that's all right."

"She's comin' over here." He had his helmet on. He took it off.

"I don't mind."

Wilda was tired and her throat was caked with travel dust. But she leaned forward and her eyes darted as she said, "I'm looking for Paul Schuen. Do you—"

"Paul Schuen? Sure."

"Wait a minute, Al. Can we help you, lady?"

"Yes. Take me to Mr. Schuen. I'm his wife."

Water seemed on fire in the harbor. The air and water were still together, nothing moving except the heavy heat bearing down on the ships and the fishing boats moving out on the flaming surface. On one big white steamer the gangplank was taken up, the water swirled about the sides, and the only sound now was the great propeller throbbing through the still water.

"Let's go in the cabin."

"Don't you want to watch—take a last look?"

"No, I saw enough of it. Let's go in the cabin."

"All right."

Then, in their cabin, he was saying, "I'm going to make up for this. If I can't make up for it there's no use living."

"You're making up for it now. You're with me, aren't you? That's all I want."

"What should we do, Wilda? What can we do?"

"We can live." She put her arms around his neck, rested her chin on his shoulder as they looked out through the porthole, and saw the clustered river boats, the jammed river dwellings, little figures moving about convulsively, silhouetted against the widening band of sun-washed water. But these people were still alive, and like all humans, they were making their frenzied retreat from death and darkness.

"Yes," he said, slowly, turning his eyes away from the receding land, and lowering them to her eyes, "that's about all we can do, isn't it?"

The big white steamer moved steadily out to open sea.

CHAPTER XXIII

Contrary to his expectations, Paul received no little notoriety when he arrived in the United States. He was the subject of a score of feature stories in San Francisco, and the newsreels played him up big. He was besieged by ghost writers and a few press agents, and finally accepted an offer to have his name used as the author of a series entitled, "I Felt Like Fighting." A smart publicity man signed him up for vaudeville appearances in small towns, where he was to stand at the side of the stage and explain various air maneuvers shown on the screen. Other projects followed. Magazine articles, lectures, advertising testimonials, and finally, as a result of the growing publicity, he got a good ground job with a big outfit, and the press agents managed to repeat again and again the story of the man who had come back from flying bombers through battle-smeared China skies to a post of peacetime aviation in peaceful America.

His first week back in New York was a very busy one, and he got very little sleep. He was called upon for lectures, luncheons, banquets, and propaganda meetings. The latter he shunned. He wrote one of the groups a long letter explaining that he had not gone to China to fight for a cause, unless mercenary motives could be called a cause. The group wrote back emphatically stating that it made no difference, he had spilled his blood for a free China. Paul replied that this matter of spilling blood was strictly involuntary, and would they please leave him alone?

But he did find time to arrange a meeting with Herb. It was a quiet meeting in a quiet place, the quiet bar where not so long ago they had started out on a big evening together. They reminisced about it, and Paul smiled, and then chuckled for an instant, remembering, trying to remember.

"We ended up there at that girl's place—gee, I forget what she looked like. But she was a sweet kid, wasn't she? I don't even remember, to tell the truth."

Words came easily from Paul's smiling mouth. He's happy, thought

Herb. He's back again and he's happy. He looks good, too. He's bigger, he even looks younger. He's back again with Wilda.

They did not talk very much, because Paul was waiting for Herb to ask him questions and Herb was not asking. Finally Paul said, "You'll want to know about Jean."

"No, I won't."

"But after all—"

"It's over and done with. She's dead and that means it's all over."

"Yes, but—" No, I can't tell him that. He's right. It's over and done with. It's all over now.

"Let's go out. You don't want to start drinking."

"That's right. Well, one or two won't hurt."

"Nothing doing. Come on, soldier."

Paul laughed. He followed Herb out of the place. They went over to Paul's apartment. Wilda was there, and when she saw Herb and Paul her face took on a gleam of thankfulness, and then she looked at Herb with triumph in her eyes, but triumph somehow devoid of selfishness, so that as he left a little while later, Herb remembered that expression on her face, on both their faces as they looked at each other. Wilda and Paul.

Then it was just a matter of taking a dive and coming up again, taking another dive and coming up again. Only sometimes when a guy came up he didn't come up far enough to take another dive. And sometimes he didn't come up at all.

Scram, Dorothy, scram out of my head, will you? Go on, angelface, you've been there all day long. Leave me alone for a while. Take a walk.

Splashing in his face, the water streamed down his cheeks and over his chin. Cold and wet in his eyes, darting, cutting wet through his skin and lips, the cold water made him jump up. Helen was standing in front of the chair with an empty glass in her hand.

"Now," she said.

"Oh. I needed that bad."

"I know you did. That's why I gave it to you."

"Go on and laugh, if it's funny."

"It's not funny," she said.

"Come on, let's go out, let's do something. What do you want to do?"

"I don't feel like going out, Herb."

"Now what's ailing you?"

"Herb," she said, looking away from him, "let's break this up."

"Why?"

"I'm tired of throwing cold water in your face."

"Is it that bad?" He took her arms and turned her so that he could look into eyes trying to avoid his.

"Yes," she said, after a moment. "I notice it during the day, in the office. You don't realize. But you're sitting at your desk, and you're in a fog. And I can talk to you and talk to you and you don't hear me. And in the night it's worse. Last night you were talking in your sleep."

"What did I say?"

"Enough."

He had a towel to his face, and his eyes were blinking out water. He said, "All right, from now on I'll be good."

"No, it's better that I go. Listen, Herb, some day you're going to find that girl. And by that time it may be a real job for me to pick myself up and make a gracious exit, because I don't exactly detest you, you know. And when you find her—"

"I'll never find her."

"Yes, you will."

"I'm saying that—well, would you marry me?"

"Is that a proposal?"

"What does it look like?" He had to smile.

"It looks like you're strictly from London, surrounded by a fog, and walking into trees. No, I wouldn't marry you. I'd like to very much, but I wouldn't."

"That sounds sort of final."

"It is final." She came up to him and pushed him back against the sofa. She lowered herself to him, pressing his head back into the soft pillow, and then moved her lips up and down on his. "Did you hear what I said? It's final." Then she was unbuttoning his shirt and moving her hands around his chest and ribs.

Then after a while she said, "At least we're a little happy this way, Herb. But if we were married, we wouldn't be. Now say that I'm right. Say it."

"You're right."

"Is anything more important than being happy?"

"No—unless it's—making others happy."

"Then shut up, and you'll make me happy."

"If—"

"Shut up."

They went to sleep that way, and he could hardly get a word in. But before they fell asleep, he made her promise that she would stay here a little while longer with him.

CHAPTER XXIV

For two weeks more Helen lived in the apartment. Then she found a few nice rooms conveniently situated and one of the girls from the office moved in with her. This other girl was fun-loving and laughed most of the time, and although she was shallow, Helen was glad of it, because she needed the companionship of someone like that.

This girl introduced some of her gentlemen friends to Helen and one of them turned out to be a clean-cut radio engineer. He was thirty-six and had been married once. He liked Helen a lot and he began seeing her. Every time she saw him she liked him more. One day he told her all about himself and wound up by saying that he wanted her to be his wife. She told him that she would think it over.

There was something about this man that told her he would do his utmost to make her happy. He was more on the quiet side, but he could talk and he could laugh, and of one thing she was sure, he was no faker. He had this very good job in radio, and he was clean and dressed well, and perhaps he could even be thrilling after a while.

In the office she told Herb about it. She said, "I'm going to be married." Oh, Norman, Norman ...

"I'm very glad. Really I am."

"I know you are," she said.

"You won't be working here anymore, I suppose."

"No. But I'll still be working. He's getting me a better job. Easier, more pay. He's very nice, Herb. I want you to meet him."

In a few days she was gone. He would see her once in a while, on the street, in a restaurant with her husband, in the foyer of a theatre, but only for a minute. He would really never see her again.

The girl who took Helen's place was tall, very thin, and had a perpetually unfriendly light in her eye. Right off the reel she started fireworks with Herb and began giving him trouble. She had the bad habit of assuming things, and once when he accidentally brushed her side going past her, she said, "I beg your pardon," and drew herself up like a crane.

"No offense. Sorry. It was an accident."

"Mr. Hervey, we might as well understand a few things here and now."

"They're understood already. Will you take a letter?"

"Mr. Hervey, am I going to be safe in here with you?"

He took a long look at that face. "I'm certain that you will be. Will you take a letter?"

In a way something like this was good for him. The girl was none too intelligent, and she was slow. She was so self-conscious that some of the things she did, and some of the statements she made were really funny. He would never laugh outright at her, and he went out of his way to cater to her desire for decorum and courtesy. But inwardly he got a big kick out of her daily struggle against the universe and mankind.

Then the days began to flick by and September was coming to an end. The work came in each day, and he applied himself to it, and then met a friend in town, or took in a movie. Then he went back to his apartment, alone, and read or thought himself to sleep.

It was getting so that this nightly thinking rite might have been planned for him and placed upon his life schedule. The room dark around him, the lights from the street blinking and bouncing up against the walls and ceiling, he opened his eyes as if slowly arising from a calm lake. Slowly then, as he arose, she would be there, and there was nothing to do but think of her and wish for her.

No clues, nothing. She might be in this city, she might be a block away from him at this minute. But how was he to know? He did not know her last name, he knew nothing at all of her former address, her former life.

He fell asleep in the same way he would fall bumping down a flight of stairs and the next day at work he could not concentrate. While he was working with this new girl he let his words fade away and forgot that he was in this room supposed to be working, but now staring at the floor.

"Mr. Hervey."

He heard a droning far away.

"Mr. Hervey."

He looked up. "Oh."

"I got a lot of work to do, Mr. Hervey."

"Sure, sure, we'll get this over and done with in no time."

You'll have to cut this out, he told himself. Now I mean it. Cut it out.

Paul and Wilda had him over at their place a few times for dinner and they were in a new, larger and finer apartment now. Paul was doing very well and the first impression Herb received when he came in was one of comfort. Added to this there was a decided aspect of luxury. But greater than either of these, or both combined, was the way Paul and Wilda looked at each other, talked to each other.

When Herb left their place he said to himself, Well, I'm glad everybody's happy. But while early fall wind cut across his eyes as he walked on the wide uptown pavement, he knew that the gladness was nothing more than a thin covering which would soon be torn by feelings which centered toward himself, his own thoughts, the things which were happening to him, what she was doing to him.

Where are you, where are you?

Well, what was going to happen? Was this going to last forever? Was it going to keep up like this, get worse every day? Was this to be his life, for the rest of his life to have her in his mind all day, all night?

No, it isn't that bad. Don't tell yourself it's that bad. Don't make it worse than it is. But it's bad enough.

Then he would try to rationalize, and at times he would try to talk himself out of it. Some nights he would smoke and read, then find himself staring out at the other side of the room, where the lamp glow was weak, and darkness edged with yellow rings crept along the wall. He would be staring there, the book would be closed on the bed, on the floor, the smoke from an unpuffed cigarette curling slowly past his mouth, nose, eyes and he would be staring and thinking of her.

If I thought for one minute that travel would help, I'd go away right now. I'd get up out of bed and leave. Just like that. But I'd see her in Africa, I'd see her in Alaska. I'd see her anywhere and anytime. Why can't I really see her? Why are you sitting in bed here like a sap and doing nothing about it? Do something. Get out of bed. Go downstairs. Get out on the street and look for her. Run along the road in the country, look for her. Swim rivers, look, look. She's someplace. She's someplace right now, breathing, sleeping, tomorrow she's going to wake up just like you and go through the same day, the same hours of the same day, just like you. So she's somewhere, she's got to be someplace, and well now tomorrow she wakes up just like I wake up and where does she wake up? In what house? In what street? In what city? This city? It's a big town. Why does it have to be such a big town?

His arm went up and flicked out the light. He let himself fall back and his head met the back of the bed instead of the pillow. The sound was a hollow conk. It hurt and he grinned and rubbed his head. Maybe if he hit it hard enough he would knock himself out and then he would be able to sleep. Or maybe he was falling asleep now. Think of something, think of something. A guy in a green jersey, from Dartmouth, smashing through center on his own thirty-yard line and going straight through, almost in a straight line seventy yards, straight line down—

She was good to him tonight. She let him go to sleep.

But he was not good to her.

Dorothy got up out of bed and turned on the light. She put on her slippers and then she stopped and asked herself where did she think she was going? She answered herself too quickly, saying, anyplace, I don't care. Tonight she had been out for the twentieth time with the young but not so very young real-estate executive who after all was even older than Herb, two years older. He was thirty-five, and Herb was about thirty-three. Herb was young. Herb was very young, then. What was Herb doing? Where was he? I know where you are, Herb. Do you want to see me? No, you don't. But I want to see you. I'm blaming you because I can't sleep tonight. And I was thinking about you yesterday too and the day before that, you hateful thing, you. What are you doing now? Oh, Herb, I had a rotten time with that tall drink of water tonight. He says one thing over and over, and he puts it on something terrible. They all do, anyway, most of them. But so do I. I'm no good too, just like them. But I have to put on the dog, Herb, really I do. Now, no excuses. But heavens, look, it's getting cold. Soon it'll be winter. Think of that. Hmm. Winter. Cold then. Will you be cold this winter, Tommy? No, no, not tonight, Tommy, I don't want you tonight. No, please don't, dear. I mean it, I'm not kidding. Now don't. Tommy, I'll get good and angry. Be a good boy. And you too, Herb. Yes, you too. Who do you think you are? Where are you? I know where you are, but you don't know where I am, and sticks and stones can break my bones and you don't know where I am and names can never hurt me. But do you want to know where I am? And so if I told you would you come up here say hello, you. And I'd say Oh, hello. How are you? Oh, I'm all right, how are you? Oh, I'm all right. What have you been doing? Oh, not much; what have you been doing? Oh, not much. And how are you? Oh, I'm all right. How are you?

She was going downstairs and she was putting on a tweed coat over her pajamas. Then she was taking the coat off.

I'm yellow, that's what I am. No guts. But it won't be anything to laugh at if your darling wife Jean is back with you, as she probably is; and then I'll barge in, and will I be welcome or will I be welcome, at two o'clock in the morning. Oh, how nice of you to come, will you stay for tea—no, will you stay for breakfast, we have some delicious sulphuric acid with marmalade!

Out on the street a man walked alone. Dorothy's eyes followed him until he turned the corner, his shoulder emblazoned for the instant by the last dragging glare of the lamp post. Slowly she turned from the window and walked back up the stairs.

No, I know about you, Herb. I know that you're all alone tonight and why do I know? I don't know, but I just know, that's all, and don't bother me anymore. I want to go to sleep. Now I told you once, and if you keep it up, Mister, I'll haul off and give you one in the mouth that you'll remember for a long time to come. Herb. Herb. Look at that. I tell him to go away and then I call him back. I am calling you. Come here, I want you. Come here. Don't make me call you twice. All right, no dessert tonight. I guess you think you're smart.

In her room Dorothy closed her eyes.

If you need me you know where to call me.

I need you.

Then call me.

No. Just for spite no. No. No.

If you need me you know where to call me.

She opened her eyes, but the darkness was even thicker now than when her eyes were closed. And it was a glassy, blurred darkness, rippled through with spheres of wetness that collapsed and spread into vague pools, and then flowed down her cheeks.

You're such a nasty thing. Look what you're doing, you're making me cry. Would I do that to you? Just for spite I didn't call you and not only that I'll get even with you when I see you I'll make you cry, because I don't like you. I don't like you. Tommy, do I like Herb? No, see what Tommy says. He says, Dorothy, you don't like Herb. Dorothy, you love Herb. Do I, Tommy? Do I love him? Yes, Dorothy, you love him, and I want you to love him because I'm telling you that he's all right, and I want you to love him. Tommy, are you telling me that he's all right? Are you telling me? Now don't you listen in on this, you Herb, you. This is between Tommy and me. Don't you go sneaking around trying to listen in. Tommy, what were you saying? What were you telling me? Oh, I know. You were telling me

Again her eyes were closed. The last tear dried on her cheeks, and her lips were formed into a faint smile. Asleep or awake, she had not smiled like this for a long time.

CHAPTER XXV

On Sundays a man who lives by himself in Manhattan can do a lot of things. He can sleep late, he can visit friends, he can try out some early fall golf, he can go out and get in an all-day game of chance with cards or dice, he can get in his car and take a drive in the country.

Usually, on Sundays Herb got up late, about one o'clock. He would go out and eat a big breakfast, and then come back to the apartment with the *New York Times*. He would begin with the rotogravure section, and from there switch over to the news section to look over the ads. Then would come sports, the weekly summary of news, and finally the theatre. Finished with the paper, he would mope about the apartment wondering what he should do today.

This was fall, then, and on the trees lining the clean wide sidewalks which bordered the clean tall apartment buildings, there was beginning the color transformation from weak yellow green to darker green juggling hazy masses of brown and red brown. Looking out at the leaves several stories beneath him, Herb could see the light and abrupt shadow brought on by a strong sun, determined to make this a clear, glowing day.

It was a shame to be inside on a day like this. The car was full of gas. It was waiting for him. He did not know that he sighed as he took his tweed sports coat from the hanger.

It was a shame that he felt so good. It made little difference whether a man's emotion controlled his digestion, or vice versa. Herb felt clear and light inside. There was a slightly biting, clean mint taste in his mouth from toothpaste. His head was steady, he felt ready to do something. But there was nothing special to do. Right now he could go out and play nine innings of fastball. He could go out for a walk and walk twenty miles. Maybe forty. Maybe a hundred. Someday he was going to try that—walk a hundred miles over hills and meadows.

Why not? Any good reason why not?

Any good reason for not doing anything, so long as you wanted to do it? If you feel like doing something, do it, do it just at that instant when the urge is greatest. Don't you want to live anymore? You really feel like not living anymore? Kill yourself. You won't be sorry afterwards.

He opened the bureau drawer and his hand moved out to grip the automatic. There was no gun. What had happened to that gun? He needed a gun up here. That was why he had bought it about a year ago. No matter where a man lived, on the sixth floor of an apartment house or in a North Woods cabin, he always needed a knife or a rifle or a pistol.

This was one for the books. Not only had his chum George Green shot him, he had also stolen the automatic. Oh, no. The police had it. Well, they had stolen it, then. After all it was his property. Call up the police station and say, "See here, boys. You got my automatic. Send it up here in a hurry. I feel like putting one through my head."

He took off the tweed coat and threw it across the room. The best thing to do about this was to start reading the paper again. The thing was light and maybe a little comical in his mind now, but these things grew, and there was a window in this place six stories above the ground, and in the kitchen there was a gas range, and there were also neckties long enough to reach from his neck to the indirect light lamps right here in the bedroom.

For a dreamy, humorous, harebrained idea these notions grew, and the first thing he knew he'd be falling or choking or passing out wondering if it was too late and then knowing it was too late, feeling sorry for himself in the last instant, perhaps going so far as to slop the whole thing up by screaming or groaning, going out valiantly holding aloft the white feather.

But he was remembering feeling almost exactly like this a few months ago, telling himself one day that after a while it gets so bad that you want to stop the whole business. There's no use trying to fight back. Things are set dead against you, and the sooner you give up the better. It's like a mile run. You're back there in seventh place—

Look how good his memory was. He grinned sitting there looking out the window and remembering that day in the office when he had told himself this and had felt it coming on stronger, getting worse each minute. And then what had happened? Jean had come in, hadn't she? What would he have done if she hadn't come in? Jean had stopped him, then. And if she had not stopped him he would never have run up against this Dorothy business, and he would not have to be wondering now if it was really worth the trouble, breathing twenty-four hours a day and working, doing several things you didn't want to do, seeing faces you didn't feel like seeing, hearing things you didn't want to hear, just for the sake of a few, too few moments of happiness, free from artificial coloring and one hundred per cent pure.

It added up to just that. Nine-tenths of the time a guy was dying a slow death of misery and dislike of himself and others, despair, hopelessness, wonder, pain, and all this swooped up to a head of a great wish for something better. All the time this cloudy day kept getting cloudier a guy was making himself feel better by telling himself that it wasn't so bad and there were suckers far worse off than he was, and just at this minute some poor devil was getting caught under the wheels of a freight train, some kid was dying of TB, so stow the yapping and be thankful you still got two eyes, two ears, and the other necessities for a full, wholesome lifetime of misery among the miserable.

There you go, he said to himself. You're off again. Before you know it these ideas are really going to get you. They're true, of course they're true, and the whole setup is nothing more than a puncture a hundred miles from the nearest gas station and no spare tire. But once these notions take a hold on you, and you do what they want you to do it'll be all done, and you won't even have the satisfaction of thinking about them, finally waving them away with weary Ned Sparks annoyance and saying, Go away, you bother me.

Herb put the tweed sports coat on again. He looked in the mirror and saw this little guy looking back at him, not very interested in him, rather like one of the bookies out at Belmont Park, looking at guys and not too interested in them, giving them the once-over and perhaps wondering, What have you got?

What have you got?

He turned away from the mirror before the answer to that question would inspire other questions, which would lead to another enjoyable bull session on the now quite boring problem of, Is it worth it? He looked in the mirror again.

All right, all right, call me a sap, call me a sucker. It's not worth it, I'm agreeing with you. But I'm bidding anyway. Do something about it. Start something. Try and stop me.

Then Herb was going out of the room, into the next room, walking toward the door. He put his hand on the knob, he opened the door, and then, just as he was about to step into the hall, he stopped. He hesitated for the slice of a second. It was a habit he had recently gotten into, hesitating there at the door for that waiting instant before going out.

The sound of ringing burst into his ears and he stiffened and waited.

The telephone rang again.

It rang a third time.

All right, it's ringing. Answer it.

"Hello."

"Hello."

"Is that you?"

"Is—"

"Yes, it's me. Is that you?"

"It's me," she said.

"It couldn't be anyone but you."

"Couldn't it?"

"No."

"Why not?"

"Because—I've been waiting—only for this—" He wanted to jump into the telephone and slide down through the wire to her.

"Suppose it was the wrong number."

"It's not the wrong number. That's you, and this is me. It's got to be—"

"And this is me and that's you. You're angry with me, aren't you?"

"Yes," he said.

"Very angry?"

"Yes."

"Well, now isn't that just too—"

"Where are you?" he said.

"Here."

"Tell me where you are."

"I'm here, right where I am. But I can't stay here long."

"Where are you going?"

"I have to see somebody," she said.

"I know you do. You have to see me. And—"

"What's your name?"

"Herb."

"That's funny. This guy that I'm going to see—his name is—"

"I know. His name is also Herb."

"That's right. My, you're gifted, aren't you?"

"Where are you?" he said. "Don't make me ask that anymore. I've been asking that for so long now—"

"Can you wait fifteen minutes?"

"What are you going to—"

"Wait fifteen minutes."

She hung up.

A green Victoria coupe with chromium wheels and a black canvas convertible top whisked around the corner as if someone had just given it a hard shove. At another time Herb would have wondered why they let people like that take out a license. But now he stood waiting outside the entrance to the apartment house and did not notice the car nor the turn it made until it was screeching alongside the curb, and then jolting like a bronco, stopping before his eyes. The door was being pushed open, left open, the motor left running as she jumped out of the car. She was rushing toward him and he knew it was she and that she was coming to him. That was all he wanted to know.

THE END

www.ingramcontent.com/pod-product-compliance
Lightning Source LLC
LaVergne TN
LVHW010210070526
838199LV00062B/4523